WHEN KARMA HITS 3

TYNESSA

Copyright © 2023 by Tynessa

All rights reserved.

No part of this book may be reproduced in any form or by any electronic or mechanical means, including information storage and retrieval systems, without written permission from the author, except for the use of brief quotations in a book review.

SYNOPSIS

Step into part 3 where layers of deceit and betrayal will be peeled away. Nothing is as it seems, and when the dust settles, Unique won't be the only one with a broken heart.

1

GOT ME F'D UP!

Rashad Russell

I was speechless and shocked at the same damn time. I had just stood outside my front door and watched this black ass nigga's car ride past my house. Yet, his fat ass was sitting at my table like he was at home.

I honestly didn't know what pissed me off more, the fact that he was in my house chilling and shit, or him drinking one of my beers that I had been rushing home to get to.

"Man, what the fuck you doing in my house?" I finally found my voice, and the words rushed out before I knew it. Now, when I first walked in and saw him, I started to tackle his big ass out of the chair, but the fact that I knew what kind of nigga he was and knew more than likely he had a gun on him, I knew I would more than likely end up dying before I could act out my next move.

So, to prevent myself from losing my life, I pushed that thought out of my head. Not only that, but Dyce was a big nigga, and tackling him out of the chair was something that I didn't know

I could achieve. Don't get shit twisted, I wasn't a small-ass brother and I damn sure wasn't scared to go toe to toe with him.

If he stood up and wanted to fight over Unique like a fucking man, then I would damn sure be ready to do just that. I mean, let's be real; I knew why this mothafucka was in my house and it was crazy when Unique was *my* woman. She had always been my bitch since I first stuck my dick in her and nothing was going to change that.

Not even my marriage to her best friend—which, that shit was about to be over with. I was getting my woman back. Yeah, I know I was fucked up for what I was doing behind her back, but Unique knew damn well that didn't change the love I had for her. Then, on top of that, she was carrying my child. We had always talked about a family and my fuck up wasn't going to change us being one.

Unique just had to cool off, and I was giving her time to do just that.

"Man, why the fuck you got this weak ass beer? I guess a weak ass beer for a weak ass nigga, huh?" Dyce was saying as he looked at the Icehouse bottle and downed the last of it. I opened my mouth to tell his ass not to disrespect my shit, but he let out a loud burp, stopping me from saying something. He then sat the bottle down and started moving it back and forth in his hands as his eyes remained on me.

I looked from him to the bottle, clenching my teeth. He had my ass tight about my beer. Any other time I wouldn't have given a fuck about it, but because I had started drinking more because of the shit Unique had me going through, I needed all my beers.

Looking back at his ass, I asked him again what in the fuck was he doing in my house.

"You know why the fuck I'm here. So, cut the bullshit, nigga!"

When I first walked inside, my eyes went to the sliding door and noticed it was still shut. The front door was locked, letting me know he didn't break in. So that left Unique's trifling ass.

"Man, don't tell me Nique done gave you the key to my mothafuckin' house!" I shouted out. Not exactly knowing if that was the case or not, the possibility made me angry, though. "I mean, come on, now. How else would his big ass get in if all the doors were locked? It wasn't like his ass came through the window."

This bullshit had Unique's name all over it, and I couldn't wait until he left so I can call her and go the fuck off.

No matter what I did to her, the way she was clearly trying to set me up was on a whole different level of griminess.

"It doesn't matter how I got in this mothafucka... I'm in!" Dyce snapped me out of my thoughts when he stated that.

"Yeah, clearly you'll feel that way, being that you're here for this setup and Nique—"

"Set up?" His words shot out as his head jerked back. The look on his face said that I was crazy for even thinking I had been set up. Then, it quickly turned into an amusing expression as he started laughing. Man, I really hated this nigga with a passion. I had always known he was the cocky type, but now that I knew he was fucking with Unique, it seemed he had gotten cockier. I guess his black ass thought he had one up on me or something, not knowing Unique was mine and would always be mine.

Yeah, he could play with her for right now since she was mad at a nigga, but once I got this divorce from Beauti, the shit they had going on was going to be over and done with.

"Look..."

"Nah, bitch ass nigga, you look..." Dyce cut me off as he slowly stood from the chair. We scowled at one another through challenging eyes, and I hated like a mothafucka that I was the one that blinked first. The last thing I wanted was his ass to think that I was a weak ass nigga that couldn't even hold a stare with him, because I damn sure wasn't that.

I might not have been a bigger drug dealer than his ass, but I had made a name for myself and there wasn't a doubt in my mind that he hadn't heard about me.

Walking up on me, he got all in my space. Another thing I hated was his height. He was taller than me by a few inches, making me have to look up at his big ass like I was his son or some shit. Yet, I kept my same facial expression, letting his ass know he didn't intimidate me one bit.

"I've been letting a lot of shit slide when it comes to you and Nique, but—"

"Hold the fuck up..." My head jerked back as a baffled expression coated my face. Yeah, he confused me and caught me off guard with that shit. "First of all, who the fuck are you to let some shit slide when it comes to me and my—"

"Nigga, you and your nothing! And, you know who the fuck I am..." He pulled up his pants like he was ready to fight, causing me to ball my fist up and prepare myself to go blow for blow with him. I had the urge to swing first but I didn't, and just waited for his next move. "Now, I let you slide with raping her because she damn near begged a nigga to not come over here and off your goofy ass."

"Man, I ain't rape no mothafuckin' body, but I guess she wants you to think that instead of her being a hoe that would come home and fuck her man right after being laid up with you." I laughed, knowing it would get under his skin, but my laughter came to a sudden stop when I was head-butted.

It happened so fast that I didn't even see it come. The shit nearly knocked me out. I felt myself going down but was snatched back up. Instantly, my head started spinning, and I felt the blood running down my face.

"I don't know what kind of fuck shit you on, but if you know what's good for you, you'll leave Nique the fuck out of it. Now, like I said, I let you slide with fucking her against her will, even though

I wanna kill yo' ass right now for it, but you trying to send her back to prison is crossing the fucking line."

"Man, what... What the fuck you talking about? I ain't tryna send Nique back to prison."

"Nigga, I'll break yo' fucking neck if you stand here and lie to me." When he brought his hand up to my neck, I stopped him.

"Whoa... Whoa..." I threw up my hands, scared that he would live up to his threat. As I stated many times, I wasn't scared of his big ass, but at the same time, right now I was helpless. My head was killing me from when his fat ass head slammed against it and now, he had my ass yoked up like I was his damn child... his bitch, or some shit. "Man, I put it on my life that I'm not trying to send her back to prison. I don't even know what you talking about or why you would even think I am. Nique's pregnant with my fucking child. Why in the fuck would I try to send her back there?"

My vision was still a little blurry from the headbutt, but not that much where I couldn't see that his facial expression had changed up a little. The nigga didn't know about Unique being pregnant by me and it showed on his face... or, he just didn't know about her being pregnant at all and was now thinking it was his baby.

Nah, I couldn't even make myself believe that Unique was sleeping with us both without a condom. The baby she was carrying was mine, and that was all there was to it. I didn't give a fuck who she slept with behind my back; Unique wouldn't let no other man get her pregnant.

Seeing that the news of her carrying my child clearly bothered him, I rubbed it in his face some more. "I would never do the mother of my child like that. Man, I don't give a fuck what we're going through. I'm not going to have her giving birth locked up. So, I don't know what the fuck you're talking about."

Dyce tilted his head to the side as he continued glaring at me. Hatred filled his eyes again as the hard mug went back to his face, but I could still see how much the news I had just revealed affected him.

Letting me go, causing me to fall back on the arm of the couch, Dyce ran his hand over his face as I jumped up, hiking up my pants and ready to go off in his shit had he tried the same bullshit on me. I damn sure wasn't about to give him another opportunity to do that shit again.

"Listen..." His face was serious as his brows lifted. "If I find out your bitch ass is lying about trying to have my Shawty locked up, I'm killing yo' ass and I put that on my fucking life!" Just as the words left his mouth, he hauled back and punched the shit out of me, catching me off guard again.

I felt like a bitch that I couldn't even swing back due to my hand shooting up to my nose. Just like with my forehead, I felt the blood oozing out, and the pain was out of this mothafuckin' world. There was no doubt in my mind that my shit was broken.

"Damn, nigga... You just gon' sucker punch me like that?" I stated through the pain, scowling at his ass. I wanted to beat the fuck out of this nigga, but the pain wouldn't even allow me to right now. The way he had just snuck my ass, I was damn sure I probably would've gotten my ass beat, and I wasn't about to give him the satisfaction of kicking me while I was already down.

"Nah, nigga, that wasn't a sucker punch. You had plenty of chances to swing on me after I busted your shit open." He nodded toward my head, calling himself picking at the damage he'd done. "That was just me letting yo' ass know not to try no slick shit when it comes to mine. But I tell you what; if you feel like I sucker punched you, then square up with me now. Here's your fucking chance to get yo' lick back!" Snatching up his pants again, he balled up his fist and got in a fighting stance, glaring at my ass like he was expecting me to do the same. "Hit me, nigga, so I can break your fucking jaw!"

I wasn't even in the mood to fight his big ass. I mean, what the fuck could I possibly do to him right now? I was already standing here bloody with a banging ass headache and a broken nose. So, no, I wasn't about to fight him in the shape I was in.

That was like me asking him to beat my ass.

"Man, you got it, Dyce. I ain't even trying to fight you right now, bruh. You got it!" I threw up my free hand, knowing I couldn't remove the other one from my nose. My shit was bleeding too damn bad. Plus, it felt like had I stopped applying pressure to it, it would fall off. I didn't know what the fuck his gorilla hand had done to my shit.

"Yeah, 'cause you know I'll kill yo' ass in here! Now, you better get off that bullshit you on when it comes to Unique because if I have to come back to this mothafucka, it ain't gon' be no talking. A'ight?" If he thought I was about to be on some, *yes sir*, bullshit, then he had another thought coming. I didn't say shit, but I guess he took that as me agreeing or something because after calling me a bitch ass nigga, he walked out my front door.

I was livid and wanted to go to the back room and grab my gun and go after his ass, but I push the shit to the back of my mind, knowing there would be a later day. I had plenty of time to kill his ass. Right now, I needed to go clean myself up and put some ice on my nose.

After wetting a washcloth, I stood in the mirror, still covering my nose as I cleaned my face. When I finally got the bleeding on my forehead somewhat under control, I slowly removed my hand from my nose and my shit was crooked. That shit pissed me off even more because even though I already felt like it was broken, I knew for sure it was.

"Fuck!" I cursed aloud as I dabbled at the blood. Now I knew I really had to kill Dyce's black ass. There was no way in hell I was about to let him get away with this shit and it angered me, too, that Unique might've been the one that let him in my house.

As I thought about that, I walked back up front to check my

doors to see if there was any forced entrance, and it wasn't—meaning Unique had given him the key to my shit.

"Bitch!" I yelled as I flopped down onto the couch after getting my phone out of my front pocket. "I got something for your hoe ass!"

As I got ready to call Unique, my phone vibrated in my hand. When I saw it was Beauti, I sent her ass straight to the voicemail because I didn't have time for her bullshit right now. More than likely, she wanted to talk about the divorce and my ass wasn't trying to have that conversation because, whether or not she wanted it, it was happening. I loved her, but I loved Unique more.

Not only did I love Unique more, but I owed her so much. She didn't only take a charge for me, but she had given me years of her best life. She had been faithful to me and always put me above anyone else. Me and Unique had always talked about getting married and what did my dumbass do?

Go out and marry her best friend.

At the time, I felt in my heart that it was the right thing to do. Beauti wasn't only pregnant with my twins, but I loved her, too. When Unique got locked up and we started spending more time together, I convinced myself that she was *the one*... That my love had grown stronger for her than it had ever been for Unique, only for Unique to get out and I realized I could never love Beauti or no other woman nearly as much as I loved her.

Unique was and would always be my number one... *my entire world*. That was the exact reason I was getting this divorce, so I could make her happy again.

She was so fucking genuine and didn't deserve what I had done behind her back. To be honest, Unique was too good for a nigga and with me knowing she was, it should've been easy for me to let her go and be happy with someone else, but it wasn't.

I didn't want to see her happy with anyone, especially that buff ass nigga. He didn't deserve her and no matter what I had done; I knew he couldn't love her the way I could. Yeah, it might've been fucked up for me to feel that way, but I couldn't help it, and deep down, I really felt in my heart that she knew that, too.

Before Unique got locked up, she never had to question my love for her and no lie; had Beauti not seduced me that night at the apartment me and Unique shared, this wouldn't have been my life.

After blowing up Unique's phone and leaving her voicemails cursing her the fuck out and a few text messages and messages on Facebook, it finally hit me that I had broken her phone. All I could do was shake my head and tell myself that, at least, she would have the messages once she got another one.

One thing I knew about her, Unique wasn't about to go too long without a phone.

Before getting up from the couch, I sent her another message on Facebook and told her that if she wanted me to get her another phone, then I would. I even told her she could come back at her car, just so I could get her back to this house, feeling in my heart that if I saw her, I could persuade her to come back home to me.

My heart refused to believe me and Unique was about to end like this.

After a while of sitting on the couch, reflecting on my life, I got a shower and headed out of the house. My nose and head were no longer bleeding, and I was going to my mama's house. I decided I was just going to chill at her spot in case Dyce wanted to come back. Before I left home, I was sure to grab my gun, just in case. Since I saw what type of time he was on, I made a vow to myself to never leave home without it again.

I had never had any type of beef in the streets, so it had been plenty of times when I would leave home without it, especially now with all the bullshit I was going through.

When I pulled up at my parents' house, I cursed when I saw my dad was home. I really didn't want him to know I had gotten my ass beat. Well, I wouldn't call it getting my ass beat being that the nigga only hit me twice, and both times were off guard. I wasn't prepared for either hit and that's how my ass ended up in the state I was in.

Looking in the mirror before I got out, I shook my head at the image staring back at me. Not only was I disappointed at how I had gotten caught up in some bullshit, but my overgrown ass was sitting here with a crooked nose and a big ass bandage on my forehead. The thought of just starting my engine and taking my ass back home weighed heavy on my mind, but I couldn't make myself do that.

Right now, I just wasn't trying to be alone, though I knew I could always go to my apartment with Beauti. That was one door that was always open for me. The thought of that made me smile a little, only for it to quickly fade. Being with her wasn't where I wanted to be. So, I couldn't make myself go lay up with her if I wanted to.

"Boy, what in the hell happened to your face?" My dad asked me as soon as he opened the front door for me.

I didn't even mention how my face had already swelled from my nose being broken. *Nope.* I didn't need a doctor at all to tell me that my shit was broken. It was obvious.

"Man, you wouldn't believe me if I told you," That was my response as I brushed past him. My mama heard him and was walking out of the kitchen when I walked in. I tried to dodge her and run up the stairs, but she called my name. I stopped in my tracks and turned around to face her.

Her and my dad were standing at the bottom of the steps and when she saw my face, her hands shot up to her mouth. Before she could even ask me, what happened, I embarrassedly spoke up.

"Man, me and Nique ain't together no more. It's a long story that I don't even want to talk about, and—

"Wait... So, Nique did this to you?" My mama cut me off,

causing me to frown as my eyes shifted over to my dad, who was looking shocked. From his expression, I could tell he was thinking the same thing.

"Nah, Nique ain't do this to me." I chuckled, but no lie; my eye was still a little black from when she had punched me in it the other day. I wasn't going to tell them she did that, though. "Nique been fucking with some other nigga, and she had his ass run up in my house."

"What?" my mom and dad shouted.

"Yeah… Well, she didn't even have him run up in my house. She gave the nigga the key," I explained. It was hard for me to believe that, but it was the only thing that made sense.

"That doesn't sound like Nique," my mom spoke up for Unique.

"Yeah, I don't know what happened or what's up with her talking to someone else, but I doubt she would do something like that."

"So, ya'll think I did this myself?" I asked sarcastically. "I got home, and her nigga was sitting in my house. Nique is the only one with a key. I checked my doors, and everything was still locked. Like, how else did he get in there and why the nigga she done started messing around with, of all people?" Neither of them said anything. "We got into it over him because I went through her phone and found out she was messing with him. So, I broke it and kicked her out."

My parents looked shocked as hell. They had always liked Unique, and that was the main reason I couldn't tell them about Beauti and our kids or me being married to her. As much as they loved Unique, they might disown my ass after hearing that.

"So, you just let him beat your ass? My dad spoke up, sounding pissed but like he wanted to laugh at the same time. "I just wasted my money with those boxing classes when you were younger, huh?"

"Man, that nigga snuck me."

"Well, from here, it looks like he beat your ass!"

"Okay... Okay..." my mom spoke up, saving me from further embarrassment. "You need to go to the hospital, baby. I can take you or—"

"Nah, I'll be okay. I'll just go—" She told me again that I needed to go now, but I declined and told her that I was just going upstairs and lay down. Right now, I just wanted to take a couple of the PM pills I had picked up for the pain, and sleep the rest of the day and night away.

I couldn't wait to talk to Unique because her and her nigga, both, had me fucked up.

2

A GAMBLE WORTH TAKING!

Dyce Walker

After leaving that nigga's house, I walked down the street to Brick's house and called Ta, who had taken my car for a spin to make shit look good on my end. I had instructed him to drive off in it when he saw Shad pull up. Shad was so fucking dumb and careless that he could easily make himself an easy target. I didn't even know much about him, but I could look at his ass and tell he was a bitch ass nigga that wanted to be hard.

That was part of the reason I didn't let him be a part of my empire a few years ago when Ta came to me about him. No lie, I told him to give me a week to think about it, but the next day after doing a little research on his ass, I flat out told Ta, no, and didn't feel I needed to give him an explanation for my answer.

I didn't really find out anything when I researched him, but it was just something about his ass that prevented me from working with him, and I was glad it was. He was too damn careless for me. No matter how tough a mothafucka thought they were in the street, the number one rule is to still not leave your house without making sure the shit is locked up—which, that was just common sense, anyway.

I was good at picking locks and my first intent was to pick his. However, when I walked around back and got ready to pick the lock to the sliding door, I checked it first and discovered that the sorry bastard had left it unlocked. All I could do was chuckle to myself and welcome myself inside. I looked around, picking up pictures and shit of him and Unique.

I honestly didn't see what she saw in that bomb ass nigga, but to each its own.

That shit was over and done with now, though, because now, Shawty had her a boss for sure... Well, honestly, I didn't know about that now. Hearing that nigga say she was pregnant was mind-blowing. If it was true, I wasn't sure if I wanted to take care of another nigga's baby, especially his. Not only that, but her ass didn't even tell me she was pregnant.

"I wonder if that fuck nigga is lying?" I mumbled as I took the blunt from my mouth that I had been sitting on my porch puffing on since I got home. The sun had started going down and I was enjoying the cool breeze. The temperature was just right. Not too hot and not too cold.

Shit. Cursing to myself, as my phone vibrated on my lap, I grabbed it to see who was calling me. When I first got here, Unique called me, but I didn't answer for her. A nigga didn't even know what to say to her ass, but I knew why she was calling. I had fucked her to sleep and then left, thinking if I would've wakened her up, she would've questioned where I was going and I would've told her, straight up, to that nigga's house.

However, it wasn't her this time.

It was my ex, Jordyn, and I didn't even feel like dealing with her ass, either. My head was too fucked up with this pregnancy news that I just wanted to smoke my blunt in peace and clear my head.

It wasn't until she hung up and called right back that I went on and answered.

"Yeah?" I said as I released the smoke.

"Damn, I been blowing your phone up for days. What does a bitch have to do to talk to you? I even came by your house yesterday and this morning but—"

"Came by my house?" I repeated, frowning. She knew I didn't like anybody popping up at my crib without talking to me first, and that included her ass.

"Yeah. I'm back in Atlanta. I'll be here for a few weeks and I wanna see you, Dyce. I was calling you before I came to see if I could crash at your place while I was here so we could talk about us."

"Now you know damn well I wasn't about to let you stay at my house." I laughed out the words. "I don't even know why you were trying to set yourself up like that."

"But that would've given us time to talk about us. You used to always tell me to get help and I did. So, I was thinking—"

"I told you that a fucking year ago, Jay," I called her by the nickname that only I called her. "You didn't want no help then. All you wanted to do was club. You picked that shit over your relationship and—"

"Dyce, don't do that..."

"Do what? When I wanted you, you wanted to run the streets with Nae-Nae. You weren't trying to be in a relationship then, but I guess now you see those liquor bottles and clubs and shit ain't gon' give you good dick anytime you want and keep your ass warm at night..."

"Dyce, baby, I was young. I mean, come on now, I'm only twenty-six... You know all the shit I've been through. Losing my mom took a toll on me, baby, and you know the only way I knew how to cope was with alcohol. I explained all that shit to you."

I huffed out a deep breath and said nothing. Mainly because I knew this shit was coming. Don't get me wrong; I knew this type of behavior was common, but I had offered to get Jordyn some help. I offered to pay for her to go to therapy and everything, but she didn't want that. She wanted to club and live her best life, so I let her.

I even told her that there was no coming back, and that was something I meant. I still had much love for her, but it wasn't enough to make me want to be with her again.

"Are you at home? Can I come there and talk to you face to face?" I still didn't say anything as I pulled the last of my blunt before putting it out in the ashtray, I had sitting beside me. I always kept one outside for when I wanted to sit on the porch and smoke. "Hello? Dyce, are you home? If you're out, you can come to my hotel room so we can talk. Please. I drove all the way back here to see you." Jordyn asked again when I didn't answer her.

There was no way in hell I was about to let her come to my house, and I damn sure wasn't about to go to no damn hotel where she was.

Running my hand down my face, I huffed out a heavy breath and then told her, "Look, man, just meet me at my bar. I'm about to head that way now." My voice was filled with much aggravation when I said that. "I'm not going to be there long, either. So you better hurry up and get there."

"I'm about to leave now. I just got out of the shower before I called you. So, all I have to do is put on some clothes and head that way. I'll see you when I get there." With that, she ended the call before I could respond.

I really didn't have time for her, but I knew she would keep on bugging the hell out of me until I gave in to her. Hopefully, after tonight, she would get the hint that there would be no more of us.

Instead of going inside my house, I got in my car and headed to the bar. When I got there, it was packed as usual. Once the sun was down and mothafuckas were off work for the day, they were sure to come to my spot. I wasn't one to brag, but I constantly patted myself on the back for opening this spot up.

Walking inside, I spoke to a couple of people before a chick I used to fuck with caught my eye. As a matter of fact, it was the same female that was inside my car the day I almost hit Unique as she was crossing the street. Her name was Adriana. I had started fucking with her right after me and Jordyn broke up, but it wasn't nothing serious and she knew that.

Being that she was chilling with her girls, I just hit her with a head nod. She blew me a kiss, causing a crooked smile to display on my face. Another thing I liked about Adriana was, she was on her grown woman shit. She wasn't with the drama, and I loved that.

Had I been ready for a relationship when she came into the picture, I damn sure would've made her mine, but I wasn't and over time, we just became cool with one another that occasionally fucked.

As I made it to the bar, I waved over the bartender and told her to bring me a double shot of Hennessy. Once I had it, I went over to the side of the bar where the two pool tables were. It was some nigga I knew from around the way playing and some waiting for next. I kicked it with them for a while until my phone vibrated in my pocket.

When I got it out and saw it was Jordyn, I answered it. She told me she was at the bar, and I headed to where she was. Jordyn had always had a way of standing out from everybody else and just the sight of her caused me to lick my lips. She was sexy as fuck.

"What's up?" I asked as I walked up to her. She turned to me and smiled, then came in for a hug. I leaned down to her but didn't bother wrapping my arms around her to hug her back. She didn't care and hugged me like she was scared if she let me go, I would vanish. "You want a drink?" I asked her, testing her to see where her mind was.

"No... I just want to go somewhere and talk to you in private. Like, this music is loud as hell. Can we go to your office?"

"Yeah, man..." Turning around, I walked off and didn't have to tell her to follow me. I lead the way up to the office and once we were inside, I walked over to my desk, letting her close the door behind her. Her back was to me for a while, and I knew it was because she was locking the door. With a shake of my head, I leaned against my desk as I asked her when she turned to face me, "What's up?"

"You... Us..." By now, Jordyn was making her way to me. Being that I was standing wide-legged, she stood in between my legs. While her eyes were locked with mine, she rubbed her hands up and down my arms. "I want you back, Dyce. You're treating me like I cheated on you, and I didn't. I was dealing with something, and I can't believe you're holding it over my head."

"Man, I ain't holding a gotdamn thing over your head, Jay, and you know that."

"Yes, you are."

"No, I'm not!"

"Well, why can't I get a second chance? I don't even drink like that anymore. I might have wine or something, but that's it. I haven't been to a club in months, and I've been working on myself. Baby..." She rounded her arms around my neck as she pushed up on her tiptoes and started kissing the side of my face. There was no doubt in my mind that she felt how hard my dick instantly got for her. "I know you missed me because I'm the only one that can get this dick to get this hard. You even told me that before."

Her arm fell between us, and I allowed her to grab a hold of my dick. She massaged it through my pants and no lie; that shit felt good as fuck.

Even so, I told her, "Nah, you ain't the only one that can get it this hard no more..." I moved her hand when I said that, knowing that shit would get under her skin. I was right, too. She pressed her lips and rolled her eyes, but it wasn't like I had lied.

"Whatever... Dyce... So, what do I have to do to get you back?" She brought her arm back around my neck and asked. "Just name it. Really, I don't know what it would be being that I've already fixed what broke us up. Like, I'm dead-ass trying, Dyce. I love you, baby, and I'm ready to come back home."

"Man... Jay, I can't go back down that road with you. I have love for you, and you know that, but we'll never get back together." She sucked her teeth and snatched her arms from around my neck, then flopped down in the chair that wasn't too far behind her. She looked so hurt, but there was nothing I could do about it. "Dead ass, I'm happy for you as far as you not drinking like that no more, but I'm not even trying to be with you like that. If you want, we can be friends, but that's up to you."

"Because you done started fucking with another bitch, ain't it? That's why you can't be with me." I frowned in confusion, wondering how she even knew that. At the same time, I kind of figured she knew something because of the way she rolled her eyes seconds ago when I let her know that she wasn't the only one to get my dick to react just from a touch alone.

Even so, I played it cool. "Man, what the fuck are you talking about?"

"Don't play with me, Dyce. I know you seeing somebody else." I pulled my bottom lip into my mouth as I dimmed my eyes. If she did know something, it wouldn't take a rocket scientist for me to know who had told her, and best to believe, I was going to deal with her ass. "She's the reason I can't get my man back?"

"You the reason you can't get me back... Even if I would've been up for giving your ass another chance at the beginning of our breakup, do you really think I would still feel that way after all this time?"

"Yes!" she answered me like she knew for sure that I was sitting around waiting for her ass to come back to me. It was crazy because I thought for sure Jordyn knew me better than that. "Dyce, we were in love when we were together. We were perfect and now you about to let some bitch mess that up?"

"Aye, man. Watch yo' fucking mouth!" I warned her. No matter how I felt about Unique right now, she didn't deserve to be called out her name. "And I've already told you, me not wanting your ass ain't got shit to do with no other woman. So, chill with the extra shit."

"Yeah, you just don't want to tell me the truth, but I know the real. As much as we were in love, you mean to tell me that you no longer feel anything for me?" She paused. I guess she was expecting me to answer her, but I didn't, and that was because I didn't want to hurt her damn feelings. Standing to her feet, she walked back up to me, but this time, she didn't bother hugging me. She just stood between my legs and looked up at me. "So, you're in love with her now? I already know you been bringing her up to your office and everything, and as far as I know, I'm the only bitch you ever brought up here."

I still wasn't answering her because the shit me and Unique had going on didn't have a gotdamn thing to do with Jordyn, and I didn't like mothafuckas that shouldn't have been in my business, going back reporting what I did. I guess I should've known, eventually, that would happen.

However, when me and Jordyn broke up, I asked Nae-Nae if it would affect her working for me and she told me it wouldn't. I should've known better.

Before Jordyn moved away after we broke up, her and Nae-Nae were thick as thieves. Nae-Nae was even the one that had set us up. She was cool and everything, but because of her loyalty to her girl, I hated I didn't go with my guts and fire her ass like I wanted to, the day Unique first agreed to meet me here and she was our waitress. She gave my ass the side eye when I had her bring me and Unique something to drink.

My guts were telling me that she would go back and run her mouth, but I guess the generous side of me wanted to give her ass the benefit of the doubt.

"Look, I don't give a fuck what Nae-Nae has been telling you, but tell that hoe to stay the fuck out my gotdamn business." I paused before I let out a chuckle. "As a matter of fact, don't even worry about it. I'll take care of her."

"Hold on... Nae-Nae, ain't been telling me shit!" She looked me dead in the face and lied. "I promise you she didn't tell me anything. So, you don't even have to go and say nothing to her."

Laughing as I shook my head, I stood up straight and walked around her, heading to the door. I felt there was nothing else that needed to be addressed in my office. I told her I didn't want her ass and there was no hope of us getting back together. That was all there was to it, and now I was ready to handle some business downstairs and go home.

"Dyce, wait... We're not done talking." Jordyn told me once I opened the door and stepped aside so she could walk out first. When I didn't say anything but gave her a look that clearly said we were, she sucked her teeth and grabbed her purse off the couch she had tossed it on when she first walked inside. Instead of walking out, she stopped in front of me. "I'm not stopping until we're back together. I deserve another chance and I'm going to get that. So, whatever bitch you're seeing, she won't be in the picture long."

I told her with nothing but seriousness in my voice, "I've already told you about calling Shawty a bitch. Her name is Nique. So, anytime you address her, call her by that."

"So, you are seeing someone else?" I pulled my office door closed, knowing it would automatically lock behind me, and headed downstairs. I ignored Jordyn the whole time she walked behind me, fussing and shit about me being with someone else like there was really a chance that we would get back together. I just wanted her to get the picture.

"Dyce, listen..." Jordyn grabbed my arm. Being that I wasn't trying to be rude, I stopped walking and turned to face her. The music was loud, making me have to lean down so I could hear what she had to say. Still holding my arm, she wrapped one arm around my neck, resting her hand on the back of my head as she whispered into my ear. "I want to talk to you about something else. I was going to do it upstairs, but the conversation went left. So, can we just—"

I cut her off by motioning like I was about to walk off, only for her to grab me again and pull for me to lean back down.

"Man, what, Jordyn? Say the shit now."

"No, it's something that we need to discuss in private. I don't need a bunch of mothafuckas around when I tell you this." I stood up straight and just stared down at her, looking into her eyes to see if I could tell if she was playing games or not. Either she really had something to talk to me about, or her ass had become a pro at playing mind games.

Blowing out a heavy breath, I leaned down so that my mouth was at her ear. I said, "Look, I'll call you tomorrow or when I get time, so we could meet somewhere, but you better not be on no bullshit, Jay. I ain't playing no games with yo' ass."

"I'm not..." I leaned up to see that she was wearing a big ass smile on her face. Shaking my head, I walked off with one mission on my mind. That was to find Nae-Nae, who I knew was working.

However, I was stopped by my boy, Ta, and he had Kelsi with him. I tried not to even look at her ass because of the foul shit her and her sister were on. Yeah, Unique told me how she was a witness to her sister and Shad's wedding, and I thought that shit was fucked all the way up.

"I ain't even know you were here," Ta spoke to me as we

slapped hands and brotherly hugged. Before I could even speak up, Jordyn stepped in front of me, grinning from ear to ear as she spoke to Ta. He looked surprised but spoke back, nonetheless. He even embraced her in a sisterly hug. He had always had respect for Jordyn off the strength of me. "How you been, sis?"

"I been good... Just came back to town a couple of days ago."

"Oh, word?" Ta's eyes bucked as he looked up at me and then back at Jordyn. I was trying my damnest to not pay either of them any attention. One thing I wasn't about to do, was entertain Jordyn's ass.

What put the icing on the cake was when her crazy ass had the nerve to wrap her arms around me and say, "I'm ready to get back what belongs to me."

Everybody looked at Kelsi when she let out a grunt. It was clear she felt some type of way, but everybody ignored her ass.

I wasn't even trying to be mean or do the shit because Kelsi was sitting here, now choking on her own drink from, clearly, what Jordyn said, but I politely removed her arms from around me and told her to chill out.

"Damn, you sure you going to be able to get him back? Look like that nigga doesn't even want you touching him." Ta laughed.

"Clearly, I have a lot of work to do, but you know, I'll be back in good. You know he can't stay away from me." Her ass laughed like something was funny, not knowing she was pissing me clean off with the bullshit ass games she was playing. She was talking a lot of shit and I didn't like it. "But it was nice seeing you again, Ta. I'm about to go over there and holler at Nae-Nae..." She then turned to face me and told me not to forget to call her and then walked off.

All I could do was shake my head as Ta laughed and Kelsi mugged the shit out of me. I wasn't even looking over at her ass, but I could feel her eyes locked on me and felt the smoke brewing off her.

I continued ignoring her as me and Ta chopped it up for a few minutes. I even had a shot, and when I was done and got ready to go, I heard Kelsi mumble something.

Running my hand down my face as I turned to face her, I asked, "Aye, you got a problem or something? I've been ignoring your little, niggas ain't shit, comments since I walked over here. If you got something to say, say the shit."

As long as I had been knowing Kelsi, she had never been one to hold back her tongue. So, it didn't surprise me that she was going to say some fly shit. "I'm just trying to see where in the hell Nique is going to stand in all this, when ol' girl gets you back? Like, does she even know about her?"

I wanted to laugh in her fucking face, but I was so angry to do so. She had some gotdamn nerve to question me about anything when it came to Unique. I guess Ta could tell I didn't appreciate this shit because he tried telling her to shut up, but she cursed his ass out like she always did.

Tilting my head to the side as my eyes narrowed, I asked her, "Nah, but I bet you can't wait to tell her, huh? You ain't going to keep this in like you kept your sister being married to Shad's bitch ass and pregnant by him, are you?" She didn't like that, and I could see all over her face that she didn't. "You grimy as fuck like yo' sister and that nigga. Then want to holler about somebody knowing something? You don't give a fuck about Unique or what she knows, so don't even sit here and act like you do."

"Whoa... Your sister married to that nigga, too?" Ta asked, looking shocked as hell. Being that he said, too, that let me know he already knew she was pregnant by Shad. I wasn't even mad that he didn't tell me, because just like I told Unique, we didn't gossip about shit like that.

"Ta, bae. We'll talk about it when we get back to my place." Kelsi told him and then looked at me. "Look, all I asked was—"

"Well, don't ask shit about her... not to me!" I cut her off. "You weren't concerned about her when it came to your sister and that nigga doing her wrong. So don't be now." With that, I turned to Ta and dapped him up, telling him that I would fuck with him later before walking off.

I didn't even bother looking for Jordyn or Nae-Nae as I walked out because I didn't want to be bothered with their asses, either. Firing Nae-Nae was just going to have to wait another time.

∽

I WOKE up bright and early like I always did. The first thing I did was, grabbed my phone off the nightstand and powered it back on. I had turned it off when I made it in after leaving my spot. Unique had called after I got out of the shower and laid down. I still wasn't ready to talk to her, so I just powered my phone off and went to sleep.

Now, I was up with a clear mind and felt I could talk to her and ask her about her being pregnant. You know, ask her if the shit was even true. My ass probably been sitting here being in my feelings for no fucking reason.

Pulling up her number, I rubbed my hand down my face and then hit send. I laid on my back, staring up at the ceiling as I waited for her to pick up. When she did, she sounded like I had just woken her up, which was probably expected being that it was early as hell.

It was only a little after seven.

"You sleep?" I asked the dumbest question in the world. I hated with a passion the way she had me feeling right now. Not only was I digging her too fucking much for me to not even have known her long, but my head was fucking up by the possibility of her being pregnant by that nigga.

"Yeah, I was. I've been calling you all night. I'm glad to know you're okay."

"What makes you think I wasn't?" I wanted to know.

"I don't know." She answered through a yawn. "You weren't responding to my texts or answering my calls, so I was worried. I mean, I didn't know what to think." I didn't say anything, though I wanted to say a lot. I just didn't think asking if she was pregnant was a question that I needed to ask over the phone. Shit, it was one that I didn't even know if I wanted to know the answer to. There was no doubt in my mind that if Unique was pregnant, the baby was Shad. I never went up in her raw until yesterday and now that I thought about it, maybe she let me then because she was already pregnant. "Hello? Are you still there?"

"Yeah, I'm here."

"What are you doing? You could've woken me up and told me that you were leaving. Then you weren't even answering my calls. I hate to be a nag, but that was messed up, Dyce. Like, did I do something to make you upset the reason you—"

"Shawty..." I chuckled as I shook my head. "You ain't do shit. I just had to take care of something, and I didn't want to wake you."

"Well, I rather you had instead of just leaving me."

"It won't happen again..." There was a moment of silence between us until she asked when she could see me again. I told her right now if she wanted to and she didn't hesitate to tell me that she did. No matter how I felt right now, I wasted no time getting my ass out of bed to start getting dressed.

After showering and taking care of my hygiene, I threw on my clothes and shoes and was out the door. On the ride to the hotel, I puffed on a blunt until I was there and let the valet park my car. Her being at the expensive ass hotel made me wonder how many nights she could afford to stay here. The last thing I wanted was for her to run out of cash and have to go back to that nigga after all the pain he had caused her.

One thing I learned about Unique was that she wasn't a needy woman and before she got locked up, she liked to have her own shit. Though she had been with that lame-ass nigga for years, she wasn't the type that would ask a mothafucka to do anything for her unless she really needed it, and I loved that about her because some women wouldn't give a fuck.

They always had their hand out, expecting shit, but because I knew Unique wasn't that type, it made me want to give her the world.

The whole elevator ride to the floor she was on, I thought about what I would say once I was face to face with her. I didn't know if I should just come flat out and ask her about the shit, or what? I wasn't even sure if it was my business to ask her if she was pregnant since I already knew there was no chance the baby could be mine.

However, a nigga was digging the fuck out of her and I felt I had every right to know. That way, it would let me know where in the hell we stood when it came to us.

"Good morning." Unique was already wearing a smile when she opened the door for me, stepping aside to let me in. In response to her good morning, I pushed a weak smile on my face as I walked in, looking around as if I wasn't just here yesterday. I turned around to face her at the same time she was walking up to me. She wasted no time pushing up on her toes with her arms stretched.

We hugged and kissed. From the minty taste of her tongue, I could tell she had gotten up and gotten herself together for me.

"I'm still sleeping... Are you going to come lay down with me?" She asked, holding my hand and pulling me toward the bedroom. She didn't have to pull too hard, either. "You know I like to be held while I sleep."

I chuckled as I told her, "I got you, but you can't sleep too long. I wanna go eat breakfast and I need you to go somewhere with me."

"Okay. That's fine. I just need another hour and that's it." Her tone was dismissed, so I didn't bother saying anything else.

When we got inside the bedroom, she removed her robe, exposing her naked body, and automatically, my eyes shifted down to her stomach. I couldn't tell if she was pregnant or not, being that it was flat. So, if she was, she wasn't that far along.

"Are you just going to stare at my body, or are you going to undress and get in bed?"

My tongue ran over my bottom lip before I pushed it between my teeth. I didn't even come here with the mindset of fucking her, but now, my dick was hard as a missile, and I wanted Shawty in the worst way. *See?* This was the shit I was talking about. It was the exact reason I had to let Jordyn's ass know that she wasn't the only somebody that could get my dick hard as hell. Even if Unique's body was covered, me and my dick would still yearn for her.

"Yeah..." I chuckled to myself as I started undressing. Once I was stripped down to my boxers, I pulled the covers back, but Unique stopped me.

"Take those off, too." She pointed down at my briefs. Her eyes traveled down to my large print and then back to my eyes. "I want everything off."

"Man, Shawty. I thought you said you wanted to come in here and go back to sleep. You didn't say anything about fucking." I played it off like I didn't want her just as much as she seemingly wanted me.

On her knees, she crawled over to me, reaching for the hem of my briefs as she stretched her neck and puckered her lips for me to kiss. I aggressively grabbed her by the neck, pulled her face closer to mine, and kissed her as she pulled my briefs down low enough to free my dick.

I kissed her hard, with everything in me as my eyes squeeze shut, trying to erase the conversation I had with Shad's bitch ass. I bet that nigga couldn't wait to tell me that Unique was pregnant by him. I could look into his eyes and see that he got a thrill from revealing that. That was the exact reason he kept throwing the bullshit in my face. I couldn't even blame him, though. I mean, had she been pregnant by me, I damn sure would've done the same thing.

As our passionate kiss ceased, Unique pulled back and asked me, "Why you never asked me to give you head, Dyce?" I frowned at her question, thinking to myself that it was a crazy thing to ask. "You never hesitate to eat me out. So, why you never asked for anything in return?"

"Because I shouldn't have to ask. The fuck. I knew you were going to do it when you got ready."

"Hmmm... You think?"

"I know..."

She pushed a smile onto her face and shook her head before kissing me again. This time, it was a simple peck. One after another, before she trailed them to my neck, down my chest and stomach as she took my dick in her hand. She stroked it as she continued kissing my stomach. The anticipation was a mothafucka. Just knowing what was coming next had me eager to find out if she knew what she was doing or not... To know how far my dick could go down her throat.

"Shit," I let out a groan as I grabbed the back of her head. By now, she was kissing the head of my dick, teasing me and shit. "Girl, stop playing with me!"

Giggling, she repositioned herself into a more comfortable position on the bed. I looked down at her as she stuck her tongue out and licked from the shaft of my dick to the tip. My head automatically fell back as my eyes closed and I bit down on my bottom lip. Her tongue was so warm and wet, like the anticipation was a mothafucka for her, too.

"Mmmmm," Unique mouthed as she licked my dick again before taking as much as she could into her mouth. She pulled her head back nice and slow and repeated those steps. The third time she pushed it down her throat, she held it there but stroked the side with her wet tongue. The feeling was amazing. My hand was still on the back of her head, and I pulled her into me more until she could no longer stand it and started gagging.

I released her, allowing her to quickly move her head back before she fucked around and threw up on my shit. In no time, my dick was back in her wet mouth, and she sucked my shit like no other woman had ever done, and I had gotten some good ass head over the years.

I'm talking about; she had a nigga's toes curling and everything. Had my ass flat-out screaming like a little bitch.

"Got damn.... What the fuck, girl?" The fact that she started giggling while never missing a beat of sucking my dick had me feeling like I had to pay her back for this shit. Well, not so much of paying her back, but like I had to reward her with my tongue. "You know I'm about to eat this pussy good when you finish, right?"

Smack.

I smacked her on the hand just as the words left my mouth. She was on her knees, but her ass was up in the air. I palmed her butt cheeks as she sucked my dick, spreading them and jiggling her cheeks in my hand.

I then brought my hand to my mouth and spit on my fingertip before taking it to her ass, using my spit as lube and rubbing it between her ass cheeks. I did it again and this time when I ran my hand through her ass cheeks; I rubbed her asshole with my index finger, causing her to moan against my dick.

As she sucked my shit harder, I continued doing what I was doing until I was able to finger her ass. She was moaning loud as fuck, throwing her ass back against my hand, and even I was grunting. After a while, I took my finger out, ready to taste her pussy, but I wasn't ready for her to stop sucking my dick just yet.

So, I grabbed her, flipping her upside down while I was still standing, putting her pussy in my face. We were in a sixty-nine position, and she instantly caught on and grabbed my dick, shoving it back in her mouth. The shit we were doing was out of this world.

No, it wasn't the first time I had been in this position, but it was just something special about this time, and it turned me the fuck on in a way that a nigga couldn't even explain—in a way that had me telling Unique I was about to nut already.

"Shit, me, too, baby... Damn... Right there, baby... Please don't stop... Don't stop!" She released my dick long enough to say that, then pushed it right back down her throat. She had her arms wrapped around my legs for support, but I was holding her tight as hell, making sure she didn't go anywhere as we both released.

The fact that Unique didn't miss a beat of sucking my dick while I nutted had a nigga's knees weak, and I tasted all her juices as she let it out. For a minute, neither of us could move, but eventually, I loosen my grip on her, letting her body slide down onto the bed.

"Damn...." I mumbled in a low tone. No lie; Unique had drained the fuck out of a nigga that I wasn't even in the mood to fuck her now. I had no energy left, and all I wanted to do was lay my ass down and take a nap, and that's what I did.

After we woke up, we got dressed and headed out of the room to get something to eat. On the way to the restaurant, we made small talk. I was trying my best to ask her if she was pregnant, but I was trying to see if she would tell me. It seemed as if we talked about everything but that.

We even talked about that bitch ass nigga, Shad, and she told me that she was completely done with his ass. As I sat across from her in the restaurant, I asked her if she was sure she was done, and she told me that she was. I then asked her, "So, what's next for you? Are you trying to get a job, or what you're going to do?"

"Well, I've been filling out applications since before I even found out about him and Beauti, but nobody has called me back, yet. I guess it's a good thing, though, because I hadn't even had the time or the energy to start school." She paused, taking in a deep breath and slowly releasing it. "That man has been draining me so much that I hadn't wanted to do anything productive."

"Nah, you can't let that shit happen, Shawty," I told her. "You can't let no mothafuckin' body have that much control over you that it'll stop you from bettering yourself. You gotta boss up on that nigga and show him that none of the bullshit you went through with him affected you in any kind of way. I guarantee you that it'll break him the way he tried to break you."

She pushed the corner of her bottom lip into her mouth and looked down, only to divert her eyes back to me. "You're right, and I plan to do that. I just need to figure some shit out. Like, literally, I'm starting over from the ground up. I'm homeless, car-less... I have nothing, Dyce. Shad took everything from me!"

"You have me!" I was speaking from the heart when I told her that. Reaching across the table for her hand, she placed them in mine, and I just held them. Her head was down, and I told her to look at me. When she did, I looked her dead in her eyes and asked her, "Would you accept a gift from me?"

"What?" Her nose was scrunched up. "A gift for what?"

"It's a yes or no question, Unique." She twisted her lips from side to side before slowly telling me that she guessed she would. She even told me that I didn't have to gift her anything. "I know I don't, but I want to. I just want you to boss up on mothafuckas and to let that bitch ass nigga know that you don't need him for shit. Like, dead ass, Shawty. Even if we don't be together, I still want to see you win. Alright?"

"Okay..."

"Come on. Let's go." I had already paid the tab, so all we had to do was leave. We walked out of the restaurant and headed to get her gift from me. On the way there, Unique asked what the gift was, but I told her not to worry about it. I was a little nervous because the last thing I wanted her to think was, I was one of these sucker ass niggas that went around spending my money on women.

That wasn't the case at all. It was just her, and I had to really fuck with a person to spend money on them.

"Dyce, what... Are you about to get another car?" Unique asked me as I pulled into the car lot. My surprise for her was a new car. I knew this shit was a bit much, and I had no business buying her something as expensive as a car, but I wanted her to get back on her feet. I felt this was a start.

At least with her having her own ride, she could at least have transportation to go back and forth to school or physically look for a job. What if someone called her in for an interview? Without a car, she wouldn't even have a way to get there.

"Nah, you're about to get one."

"What?" The confused frown on her face hardened as she shook her head, trying to process what I had just said. "What do you mean, I'm about to get one? Dyce, I don't have no money, and if I did, I couldn't afford shit from this lot."

I chuckled as she looked around. "Unique, come on now, Shawty. You a smart woman. Don't play dumb, like you don't know what's going on."

She glared at me before saying, "I mean, I guess I understand what's going on, but I'm trying not to believe it. We hadn't even known one another long, so what would make you want to do something like this for me? I don't have no way to repay you for this."

"I ain't ask you for shit."

She dropped her head when I said that, still not budging to get out of my truck. Her behavior didn't surprise me. There was no doubt in my mind when I told myself I was going to get her a car when she informed me that Shad had taken hers back, that I would have to make her let me do this for her. My ass started to not even go through with this shit when he revealed that she was pregnant by him, but one thing about me, I was a man of my word.

No, I didn't tell her that I was going to get her one, but I knew I was, and that was enough. It was just one thing, this shit was a gamble, because who was to say that she was really done with his ass. Then I would be looking like a fucking fool if she wasn't and then ended up riding his ass a round in the shit I had paid for.

But this was a gamble I was willing to take.

3

UNTIL FURTHER NOTICE!

Unique James

I honestly couldn't believe I had just signed the paperwork for my own car...Well, my own freakin' Range Rover. Yes, Dyce had gotten me a Rover—one that he had suggested I get. I was trying to get something cheap once I finally agreed to let him get me a ride.

I was iffy about this. For one, we hadn't even known one another long, and to me, it was strange that he wanted to get me something as expensive as a car, and two, with the way Rashad had taken the car he'd purchased for me back, I didn't want another man buying shit else for me.

However, Dyce assured me that he would never do no *'lame'* ass shit like that, and I trusted that he wouldn't. I hated that anything this man said, I believed. Once upon a time, I was the same way with Rashad, but it took almost a year for me to get that way. For some reason, it was different with Dyce. Everything about this man seemed different than Rashad and it was making me fall harder for him than I wanted to.

Well, truthfully, I had already fallen for him, and I hated it. My heart wasn't ready to love anyone... to feel anything for another man, but it was just out of my control.

"Are you coming back to the room with me?" I asked Dyce as he opened the driver's door to my all-black Rover for me to get in. He ran his tongue over his lips and then shook his head, telling me that he had something to take care of. My face scrunched up. I didn't want to come off as a brat, but I wanted to spend some more time with him. "So, that means I won't see you no more today?"

"I don't know.... I'll have to see once I take care of my business."

"Awe... Okay. I understand." Even though I did, I still didn't like it. "I'm about to go to T-Mobile and get me another phone. I'll send you a text when I get it, so you can call me after you finish with your business. Okay?"

"A'ight." With that, Dyce leaned over and kissed me on the lips. It was just a peck that I wasn't expecting. Most times he kissed me, he was sure to slip his tongue down my throat, and I was disappointed this wasn't one of those times.

After parting ways, I pulled out of the dealership and headed straight to T-Mobile. When I bought it, using the money Rashad had been putting on my cash app, I called Dyce as soon as I hooked the phone to my radio. I was still in shock that I had a Rover, and Dyce was sure to let me put it in my name. Unlike Rashad, who had the car that he was supposed to have bought for me, in his name, making it easy for him to take it back like he had done.

I felt this was his plan all alone. Otherwise, he would've waited until I got out and taken me to get the car so I could sign the paperwork.

"What's up?" Dyce's smooth baritone voice caused a smile to form on my face. Though I had just left him, I couldn't wait to see him again—couldn't wait to lay in his arms and him hold me all night. I just wanted to feel him inside of me, kissing every inch of my body.

Gosh, I can't get enough of this man. I thought to myself as I cleared my throat and spoke.

I was just calling to let you know I got a phone. So, you can call me whenever you have time." I was praying he told me that he'd changed his mind and he would meet me back at the hotel. My prayer went unanswered when he said, "A'ight, I'll call you later on."

"Okay, and thanks again for the truck, Dyce. I really appreciate this."

"You good, Shawty." We said our goodbyes and ended the call.

It was something off with Dyce, and it scared me. He was so short with me, and I didn't like that, but I didn't ask him if there was something on his mind. I mean, after all, despite how short he was with me, look at what he'd done. It spoke volume, and that was the exact reason I just let his dryness go.

On the way to the room, my phone was going off and every time I picked it up, it was a text from Rashad coming through. I didn't bother checking them and was confused about why in the hell he was texting and calling me, knowing damn well he had broken my phone.

It was strange, but I didn't pay it any attention. I was on cloud nine right now and didn't want his ass ruining my day.

Back at the hotel, and once I had settled in, I decided to check my voicemail. There were plenty of messages from Rashad, and though I didn't want to check those, I clicked on one. He sounded so upset and I didn't even finish listening to the whole thing before ending it and calling him.

He answered the phone, ready to go off on me before I stopped him. I asked, "What in the hell are you talking about, Shad? I didn't give nobody a damn key to your house. I don't even have a key to it. Remember, you took it."

I was so heated by his accusation that I was now pacing around the living room area of the hotel room.

"You a mothafuckin' lie, because if you didn't give that fat, bitch ass nigga a key to my shit, then how in the fuck did he get in?" Rashad yelled through the phone.

"I don't know... And what are you talking about? When did he come into your house?" I knew he was talking about Dyce because he had said his name on the voicemail. None of this was making sense to me.

"The mothafucka was in my shit when I got home yesterday. Don't sit there and act like you didn't know, and if he didn't break in, then how the fuck he got in? You talking about some, I took your keys, but your slick ass probably had another one made."

"Really? Are you fucking hearing yourself? Why would I get another key made when I already had one?" I yelled, matching his attitude. I didn't like that he was accusing me of something as serious as this. "I didn't give Dyce a key to your house, and if he didn't break in, then maybe you left a door unlocked, but I didn't have shit to do with him coming to your place."

"The fat ass nigga sucker punched me while he was there, threatening me and shit. And where the fuck he get that I'm trying to send you back to prison? Where the fuck you at, at his house, pillow talking and lying and shit about me? You just over there living it up and making me look bad as fuck, huh?"

"Shad, I don't have to make you look bad, you made yourself look bad." He didn't even have a comeback to that, and I didn't blame him because it was the truth. There was nothing I could say to make his ass look any worse than he already looked. "And yes, I told him that somebody is trying to send me back to prison, and it had to have been you. I mean, you're the only one that knows I hadn't been coming home and missing my curfew. So—"

"So, you really think I would do some grimy ass shit like that?

Maybe his ass is doing whatever you trying to accuse me of doing?"

"Nah, I doubt that..." I flopped down on the couch and put him on speaker, pulling up Dyce's name in my message thread so I could text him. My heart was pounding as my hands trembled. I couldn't believe he had gone to Rashad's house.

"So, if you doubt that he would do some shit like that, what in the fuck makes you think I would? I'm the nigga that you been with for ten gotdamn years, and for you to say that I would try to send you back to prison is fucked up."

"Because I don't put shit past you, Shad! I'm the bitch that you been with for ten years and look how you did me. You married and started a family with my best fucking friend. Now you expect me to think you're not trying to send me back to prison? To be honest with you, I'm looking at you and that hoe sideways. Ya'll probably set me up the first time."

"Come on now, Nique... Don't even do that shit!" The hurt in his voice outweighed the anger. "You know I wouldn't do no shit like that. I don't give a fuck what I did. I wouldn't do that."

"Look, Shad, I have to go... I didn't have nothing to do with Dyce going to your house. Okay?"

"So, you just about to rush off the phone with me? We ain't even talked about us, yet."

"Because it ain't shit for us to talk about. That's why we haven't. Now, I'll talk to you some other time." I was trying to get off the phone with his ass so I could call Dyce. I had sent him a text when Rashad first told me that he went to his house, telling him to call me, but it was taking him too long to.

"Do you know that nigga snuck me, or you just don't give a fuck?" I asked him what he meant by, *snuck* him, refusing to believe Dyce had beaten his ass. "So, you hadn't checked your text messages? I sent you pictures. It's fucked up that his fat ass didn't even give me a fair fight. Bitch ass nigga had to catch me off guard."

I closed my eyes when I saw the damage Dyce had done to Rashad's face. While I wanted to feel sorry for him, I truly didn't and felt he had gotten what he deserved. I didn't condone any violence, but Rashad ran his mouth too much. I was glad Dyce had beat his ass, and I couldn't wait to do his bitch the same way.

"Did you look at it?" Rashad grilled me. When I told him that I did in a nonchalant tone, he went, "That shit is fucked up. You already know I'ma get at that nigga and I'm telling you that so you can tell him."

"Look, I ain't in this bullshit! I'm sorry he came to your house, but it ain't shit I can do about that, and clearly, nothing you can do about it, either."

"So, that's all you gotta say?"

"I don't know what else you want me to say. Why don't you call your wife and cry to her about what happened, because honestly, I don't want to hear the shit." There was a moment of silence as I thought about him actually being married to Beauti. Closing my eyes, I counted to ten, refusing to cry over their asses. When I reopened them and knew I had calmed down, I told him again that I had to get off the phone.

This time, I didn't even wait for him to retort anything before ending the call in his face so I could call Dyce, only for him to not answer his call. I then pulled up Mrs. Walker's number only to not hit send to call her. She was already in my mess enough and I didn't want to drag her in it any more than she already was.

Plus, the last thing I wanted was to bother her with any of my problems or to call her anytime I couldn't get in contact with Dyce.

So, I powered my phone off since Rashad was already blowing my shit up and went into the bedroom. I sat my phone on the nightstand and then stripped out of my clothes and got in bed to take a nap.

When I woke up, it was dark outside, and someone was banging on the door. I quickly snatched my phone off the nightstand only to remember that it was turned off. While it was powering back on, I looked at the time to see that it was almost ten at night.

"What the fuck?" I mumbled as I jumped out of bed and grabbed my robe that was at the foot of the bed. I couldn't even believe I had slept that long.

As I walked to the door, my heart raced as Rashad came to mind. There was no way he could've known where I was. Despite that, a bitch was scared until I looked out the peephole and saw that it was Dyce. Automatically, my nerves calmed as I snatched open the door.

As he walked in, he pushed a smile onto his face. He was no longer wearing what he was hours ago when I last saw him, and he had on a hat that was pulled down low. He looked damn good, but he smelled just like weed.

"You were in here sleep?" He asked me, staggering toward the bedroom, and I followed. I had never seen him this drunk to the point where he couldn't walk straight.

"Dyce, you're drunk?"

"Nah, a nigga ain't drunk." He even laughed when he said that as he took a seat on the bed, then fell backward. "I been drinking, but I ain't drunk!" He slurred.

"You are, drunk!" I stood in between his legs. I guess he felt me in between them because he sat up and wrapped his arms around me, palming my butt. "Why did you drive over here, and you been drinking?"

"Didn't you say you wanted to talk to me about something? You said it was important, right?"

"That doesn't mean drive over here drunk." I could barely get my words out. The man had untied my robe and was kissing my stomach. "Shhhh... Wait, Dyce... Just go to sleep, baby. You're drunk."

"I wanna fuck you right now... I'll go to sleep when I'm done."

I pushed his head back. There was no doubt that sex with him, while he was intoxicated, would be out of this world, but he was just too drunk right now. I could even smell the liquor and weed on him. "Go up there and go to sleep."

"Damn, can a nigga at least hold you, then?" He stood. I backed up some, allowing him room to move around. He went into the bathroom and while he was in there, I moved to the side of the bed where I had set my phone on the nightstand. It had chimed and when I picked it up, I saw that it was a text from Rashad.

Of course, I didn't bother checking it and just powered my phone back off. Dyce was here, and I didn't have time for his bullshit right now.

"Aye, bae... You'll do me a favor?" Dyce asked, walking out of the bathroom with his pants halfway down. He was fucked up. I know we hadn't known one another long, but I had never seen him this way. To be honest, I didn't think I would ever see him like this. Dyce was so level-headed, that I never would've imagined him to not know his limit. It didn't bother me, but at the same time, it was like, what the hell...

"What?" Getting off the bed, I walked around to where he was. "Let me help you undress and get in bed.

"I need to eat something first..."

Me thinking he was talking about eating me, I responded with, "No, Dyce. We can have sex tomorrow. Right now, you need to lay down and sleep this off."

"I wasn't talking about eating you, Unique." I heard the amusement in his voice and looked up at him. He was looking down at me with a crooked smile fixed on his face. "I was talking about food. I wanted you to order me something, but if you want me to eat that pussy, then you know I have no problem doing it. As a matter of fact, order us room service, because I know you hungry, too, and while we wait, you can sit on my face."

I didn't say anything as I stared at him as if I was considering taking him up on his offer. I wanted to, real bad, but I wanted to talk to him about the shit Rashad had told me. Dyce had no business going to that man's house. I got that he was looking out for me, but still... The last thing I wanted was for him to get into any kind of trouble behind me and my B.S.

All I needed was for him to understand that.

"How about this? I order us room service and while we wait for the food, we have a serious conversation?" He looked up at me for what seemed like forever, giving me the strangest look. Then finally, he said, okay, we could certainly do that.

After ordering us some food, me and Dyce didn't talk at all. His ass fell asleep, and I didn't wake him until the food got here. We ate in silence. Well, he did. I had too much on my mind to enjoy my food, so I eventually just put it up. I let Dyce enjoy his, though, and when he was done and got ready to make himself comfortable in bed, I spoke up.

"Dyce, why did you go to that man's house?" He was walking out of the bathroom and stopped in his tracks. He turned to face me, narrowing his eyes at my ass like I had some nerve to question him about that. "Shad called me and told me that you went to his house, starting shit with him. Like, why would you do that?"

"Why wouldn't I?"

"Because I told you that I would handle him. I made it clear that I didn't want you getting in the middle of my bullshit with Rashad and—"

"And I made it clear that I didn't want to hear none of that shit!" He cut me off. "Somebody needs to teach that mothafucka a lesson, and if he keep on with his bullshit, it's gon' be me. I already gave his ass a warning while I was at his house."

"So, you did do that to his face?" I couldn't believe Dyce had fucked up Rashad's face like that. On the inside, I just wanted to jump into his arms and kiss him with everything I had in me. I hated but loved it at the same time how hard Dyce was going for me... How he didn't play about me. Any other man would've run for the hills after finding out all the baggage that came with me, but not Dyce, and that was the part that made me fall for him so hard.

It had absolutely nothing to do with his looks—which I thought he was the most sexiest man I had ever laid eyes on. Dyce was so chocolate, tall, and handsome, and his charisma was out of this world. To be honest, I would've never expected him to be my type. Yes, he looked good as hell, as I stated, but he was the total opposite of what I was used to.

Rashad wasn't a bad-looking guy, and he was fine as hell, too... but him and Dyce were night and day, and not just when it came to their looks, either.

"Look, Unique..." Walking up to me, Dyce leaned down and kissed my lips. It seemed he had sobered up from when he first got here. "You think I want to be in this bullshit you have going on with that nigga?"

I jumped my right shoulder, as to say, I didn't know, because honestly, at this point, I didn't know what to think. No, I didn't want to believe that he wanted to be in this drama, because what sane person would, but look at the way he was behaving. I was all for him wanting to look out for me, but at the same time, I just didn't get it.

I felt it was my responsibility to get myself out of this mess, and mine alone.

"Hell, nawl, I don't want to be in this shit and if it was some other woman, I don't even know if I would be willing to put up with it."

"What makes me so different?" The words rushed out of my

mouth before I knew it, but I didn't regret my question because it was one that I damn sure wanted to know the answer to. I guess that was the part of me that was conflicted by all this; why in the hell Dyce was so comfortable about risking his freedom when it came to me?

Releasing a deep breath, he ran his hand down his face as he took a step back, eyes never leaving mine as he told me that he didn't know. He then dropped his head, shook it, and then brought it back up to look at me. "You're just different, Shawty. Like I keep telling you, I could see that you have a genuine heart, and you don't deserve the shit that mothafucka is taking you through. You're special as fuck, and now that I'm in the picture, ain't nobody about to keep playing with you and taking advantage of you."

"But, Dyce, boo…" I walked up to him, invading his personal space. "We don't even know one another that well… You don't even know me to know how special I am, just like I don't know you…" I paused, but not long enough to give him a chance to speak. Through a heavy sigh, I added, "But I do get what you're saying. As bad as I don't want to get it, I do."

"I know you do… So, please, stop questioning me about anything I do when it comes to that nigga. I'm letting you know now, if you don't want me to handle him, then stop telling me all the shit he be on."

I sucked my teeth, knowing that would be hard to do. As of now, Dyce was my only friend. Well, he was more than that to me, but he was my friend at the end of the day, and I felt I could talk to him about anything. Sure, I had talked to Mrs. Walker about what I was going through with Rashad and Beauti, but she wasn't my friend. She was the woman that had my freedom in her hands, and I felt there was certain shit that I couldn't talk to her about.

Like beating Beauti's ass.

The last thing I wanted to do was to incriminate myself in any kind of way. I was supposed to stay out of trouble and if Beauti press charges on me when I finally give her a mean beat down, then my probation officer could throw me back in jail and use what I'd vented to her about to keep my ass in there. No, I didn't feel in my heart that she would do that, but I wasn't trying to find out if she would or wouldn't.

"All I'm saying is, I wish you would've told me that you were going over there or told me this morning, that you had gone over there and beat his ass."

He didn't say anything right away as he glared down at me. Then, his next few words nearly knocked the breath out of me. He said, "Just like you should've told me that you were pregnant by that nigga."

My eyes bucked and I couldn't say shit, wondering how in the hell could he have known that I was pregnant. I damn sure hadn't told him, and I would like to think Rashad didn't—which, I wouldn't put shit past Rashad's ass. I didn't have to wonder for too long, though, because Dyce damn sure informed me how he knew.

"Yeah, that nigga told me, and I think it's fucked up that I had to hear it from him when you could've told me. I mean, you told me everything else. So, why not tell me that you're pregnant?"

I dropped my head, not even knowing what to say. I should've told him. I really wanted to, but because I was unsure if I even wanted to keep the baby, I didn't say anything.

"Damn, you don't even have anything to say now?" Dyce asked, shaking his head as he walked back over to the bed. He had stripped out of his clothes and when I saw that he had grabbed them to put back on, I rushed around to where he was and grabbed his shirt off the bed where he had tossed it while he put back on his pants.

I wasn't letting him leave. Not like this. Not only was he upset, but he had been drinking and being mad and drunk damn sure didn't mix. Plus, I wanted to talk about this and at least try to explain my reason for not telling him that I was pregnant.

"Dyce, wait... I'm not letting you leave like this," I told him. Now in his face and holding the shirt behind my back as if he couldn't take it if he really wanted it.

"Why the fuck am I staying, Nique? You just didn't have no words for me when I was trying to talk to you. So, what the fuck am I staying here for, to talk to my gotdamn self?"

"No... So we can talk!" I shouted. "So I can explain why I didn't tell you."

He tilted his head to the side and glared at me. His silence as well as the mug on his face scared me, but I played it off, not showing how afraid I was at the moment. "Are you going to stay and hear me out? I mean, really, you don't have a choice because I'm not letting you leave, and you been drinking."

"That doesn't matter, Shawty... I made it here, didn't I?"

"Yeah, and I hate you even took that risk. You were too drunk to drive here, Dyce."

In response, he took a seat on the bed, intertwining his fingers and resting his hands on his lap as he looked up at me. His eyes were fire red, and I couldn't tell if it was because he was so upset, sleepy or because he had been drinking. Despite how he was sitting, I sat on his lap, making sure he wouldn't get up and go anywhere.

He wasn't feeling my ass right now and I could tell. Not only was it written on his face and heard in his voice, but he had called me something he had never called me before. That was; *Nique*. Since I met Dyce and told him my name, he had always called me by Unique, refusing to call me by my nickname like everybody else and I had gotten used to him calling me that.

I didn't call him out on it because, in a way, I felt he had every right to be upset with me. The man had just bought me a Range Rover and the whole time, I was hiding a pregnancy from him.

However, now that I thought about it, he knew and *still* bought me the truck. That was weird but at the same time, it gave me hope that he would still fuck with me although I was pregnant by another man. There was no doubt in my mind that Rashad was the one that had informed him that I was expecting, and I knew Dyce was smart enough to know, the baby I was carrying, wasn't his.

Up until yesterday, we never not used any protection. The only reason I let him go in raw yesterday was I was already pregnant.

"I'm sorry... I should've told you I was pregnant, and I tried to tell you yesterday. I wanted to, but I just.... I just didn't know how."

"Why? All you had to do was just say the shit."

My head dropped as I mumbled, "I was scared you were going to leave and I... I needed you. I didn't realize it until you showed up at the door how much I needed you, Dyce." Bringing my head back up to look at him, I stared into those red eyes of his and then asked, "Would you have stayed if I would've told you I was pregnant by Rashad?"

This time, he dropped his head. Being that I was sitting on his lap, his hands were no longer resting on his lap, making it easy for him to run his left one over his waves as he looked away from me. My heart dropped to my stomach when he did that. I might've been uncertain if I was going to keep this baby or not, but his reaction to my question hurt to the core.

"See, that's why I was scared to tell you."

"Man...." He dragged out his word. "You still should've told me. That nigga enjoyed telling me that bullshit. Mothafucka rubbing it in my gotdamn face and shit. I didn't like that bullshit, and it almost got his ass killed."

I felt it was a little over the top for Dyce to want to kill Rashad just because he told him that I was pregnant by him. I mean, it was the truth, and that was no reason to kill the man. The way I saw it, if he was going to kill someone, it should've been me. I was the one that was obligated to tell him.

Even so, I responded with, "You're right, but another reason I didn't tell you was because I don't plan on keeping this baby. Me and you are getting along so good and I don't want—"

"Whoa... Hold the fuck up." He scowled at me. "Don't get rid of your baby because of me."

"So, if I have this baby, you would be willing to take care of another man's baby?" He didn't even have to verbally, answer me because him dropping his head said enough. "See—"

"Man, come on now. That shit would be hard as fuck for me too, especially a nigga that I despise. I definitely would have to kill his ass."

I let out a chuckle As I shook my head. "That's another reason I don't want to keep it. Well, it's the number one reason. I don't want to have to deal with Shad's ass. I don't want to be attached to him in any kind of way. Like, why in the hell would I want to keep a baby by him after what all he's done to me? I would be a damn fool and that's why I'm getting rid of it." Leaning over, I kissed his lips to assure him that my next few words were coming from the heart. I even looked him in the eyes as I added, "Baby, my decision has nothing to do with you. Of course, I want to be with you, and it scares me because I don't want to jump out of one relationship into another, but me ending this pregnancy have absolutely nothing to do with you... with us... I'm doing it because I want to move forward with my life and having a child with Rashad would only hold me back. It would have me attached to him for the rest of my life, and I don't want that."

Reaching up, Dyce stroked the side of my face as he took in a deep breath. He said nothing as he continued staring at me, looking deeply into my eyes as if he was searching for something deep within my soul. I could tell that he wanted to voice something, but he didn't, and neither did I for what seemed like forever.

Before either of us knew it, I was straddling him. I didn't even know who had kissed who first, and neither did I care. The kiss had so much meaning behind it, speaking words that both of us were scared to say. My arms were locked around his neck and the robe I had on was off me and Dyce was palming my ass as I rode his dick.

We emitted moans against each other mouths as I rocked my hips back and forth nice and slow with him matching my rhythm. When I felt his dick harden inside of me and he tightened his arms around my waist as I did his neck, I sped up my pace and started bouncing on his dick. It didn't last long because as soon as he told me that he was nutting, I slowed down as I was before and kissed him harder as I, too, reached my peak and we released together.

We both sat still as our hearts rapidly beat against one another chests. I didn't know about Dyce, but there was so much shit running through my mind... So much that I wanted to say to him, but I didn't want him to think I was crazy for expressing my feelings for him. Sure, I knew Dyce felt something for me because he was always vocal about how much he fucked with me, but I was just unsure if it equaled up to what I felt for him.

Sure, he bought me a truck and that spoke volume, but still... I just didn't know.

"Let me go get you a washcloth," I mumbled into his ear as my head laid in the crook of his neck. He said nothing, but his arms slowly unraveled from around me, allowing me to get up. After I used the bathroom, I turned on the shower for myself and started grabbing a clean washcloth so I could clean Dyce. However, he walked into the bathroom, naked.

His chocolate body was damn sure something to look at. Through the mirror, I smiled as he walked over to the toilet.

"I can get in there with you?" Dyce asked me, looking at me through the mirror. Of course, I said yes, and once we were done and cleaned, we got in the bed naked. It felt good laying in his arms, but I was restless and grabbed my phone off the nightstand and powered it back on, putting it on silent in case Rashad called.

I went to Instagram first to catch up on all the latest celebrity tea and then checked my Facebook. I had so many inboxes and I thought it was crazy that neither was from Beauti. Well, not so much as crazy, but it kind of hurt that the hoe didn't even reach out to apologize for being a grimy bitch. That let me know that she had absolutely no regret or shame in what she had done to me.

I guess it was expected, though. I mean, she had married the nigga behind my back. So, really, what explanation she could've given me?

I had a message from her mama, telling me to call her and how she didn't know nothing about Rashad and Beauti. There was a missed call from her, as well. I assumed since she couldn't get through on my phone; she called me on messenger as if I would really answer for her. Maybe I would sit down and talk to her, being that she claimed she didn't know, but right now, I didn't want to have shit to do with that family.

I also had a message from Rashad's mama, who I didn't even want to talk to right now. I knew I would talk to her before I would Mama B, though, because one thing about Rasheeda, she wouldn't condone her son's behavior. She just wasn't that type of mama. So, my heart wouldn't even make me believe she knew he had married and started a family would my supposedly had been best friend.

When I got to Kelsi's message, I started not to open it and just delete it, but my nosey ass just had to open it and wished I hadn't. I scrolled up to see what day she had sent the first message and saw it was a couple of days after I found out about her sister and Rashad. It was long as hell and I didn't even bother reading all of it because it was bullshit to me. She was basically apologizing and telling me that she was in a tough position, being that Beauti was her blood sister. *See?* I didn't want to hear all that crap because regardless of if she was her blood sister, as a woman, she should've done the right thing.

Scrolling down to the recent one she sent, it damn near brought tears to my eyes and had my ass feeling like I was about to have a heart attack as I read it twice.

Kelsi Woods:

Hey, Nique. I know you're not fucking with me, but regardless, I still love you and you're going to always be my little sister. I know it might not seem like it, but I still want the best for you and don't want anyone to bring any kind of harm your way. You've been through a lot, and I refuse to let anyone else play you. That's why I'm telling you this. It was a shocker to me being that I've put in a lot of good words for him, but sometimes I know things aren't what they seem. Before you get any closer to Dyce than you might already be, his ex is trying to get back with him, and I was at his bar and saw them come down from his office. I witnessed them whispering in one another ear and everything. He had no idea I was there until he walked over to me and Ta. I'm not telling you this to hurt you or anything, but I just want you to be careful with him. You don't deserve to be played by a no-good man a second time. You're too good of a woman for anyone to fuck over you, including, my sister. I love you and hopefully, our sisterly bond can go back to the way it was. Call me if you need to talk. I will always be here for you. I love you!

I bit down on my bottom lip as I read the message for a third time. This time, I was unable to stop my eyes from watering. How in the hell could my heart not feel some type of way after reading that?

Dyce had slowly but surely claimed a spot in my heart and I would hate for it all to end over something like this. If Kelsi was telling the truth, it would damn sure come between Dyce and me.

Now, I had to figure out how in the hell I was going to ask him about this and decide whether or not it was too soon to confront him about another woman, despite everything he had done when it came to Rashad.

Hell yeah, I have every right to question him about this. I thought, knowing there was no way I could do it right now.

I was so upset and emotional. The last thing I wanted to do was to be up in here crying and shit, and he wasn't even my man. So, when the time was right, I would ask him. As of right now, I just powered back off my phone and closed my eyes, hoping I could get some sleep while laying in Dyce's arms. The same way he had played off my pregnancy all day, I was playing this shit off until further notice.

4
LETTING IT GO!

Kelsi Woods

"Man, I still can't believe you knew yo' sister was married to that nigga and kept it from that girl? That shit is foul as fuck." I rolled my eyes as Ta stressed that for the umpteenth time since finding out that Beauti and Rashad were married, and I knew about it. It had been two days since Dyce exposed that, and his ass was still talking about it.

Even when I told him to drop it, he wouldn't. It was like he was begging me to give him more information on the situation, but I wasn't saying shit.

I didn't even want to talk about it, to be honest.

"Damn, how many times you going to say the same shit, Ta. It happened and it ain't nothing I could do about it. So let it go, please!"

I fussed, really becoming irritated with his ass. Something told me not to answer the door for him when he called this morning and told me to open up, but because I wanted to question him about where he was last night after telling me that he was going to come over and never did, I let him inside, but still didn't receive the answer I was looking for from him—which was the truth.

All he said was that he was out handling business, but when I asked what kind of business and why he didn't call me, he laughed and refused to answer. It pissed me clean off. No, Ta and I weren't a couple, but at the same time, we were doing everything that couples did. He even made it clear time after time that he wanted to be more than what we were, but I was holding back.

I guess with the shit my sister and Rashad were on, it kind of made me scared to trust men. I couldn't imagine being in Unique's shoes, to be so in love with a man only for him to shit on you the way Rashad had done her.

Knowing my ass, I would kill him and the bitch, both.

I guess that was part of the reason I was afraid to tell her about Beauti. No, I didn't give a damn what she did to Rashad, but I didn't want anything to happen to my sister, especially while she was pregnant. Had I known for sure that all Unique was going to do was beat Beauti's ass, then I would've told her because it was something that Beauti damn sure would've deserved, but I didn't put shit past a mad bitch...

A scorned woman was someone that you didn't want to fuck with. Beauti had not only gotten pregnant by the girl's man, but she married him as well. Unique had been with Rashad for ten damn years, and he didn't marry her. So, I didn't know what would've been running through her mind when she found out that he and my sister had gotten married.

I imagined myself in her shoes and things wouldn't have ended pretty. So, I was looking out for my sister, as well as Unique. Beauti would've been dead and Unique would've been spending the rest of her life in prison. I didn't want either of that to happen.

"Nawl, man... Ain't no letting it go. I been letting it go for months now. I overheard you and her snake ass talking about that nigga being her kids' dad a couple of months ago, but I didn't think nothing of it because it wasn't none of my business—"

"And it's still not your business... So, fuck you talking about?" I cut him off as I moved like I was about to get off the couch, but he grabbed me. We had been sitting on my sofa since he came inside my house, but now I was ready to open my front door and let his ass know that it was time for him to leave my house.

"It might not be any of my business, but we about to talk about this shit."

"Ta, it's nothing to talk about. I mean, damn... Her and that nigga are married. I knew and didn't say shit. Big fucking deal!"

Ta laughed as he shook his head. His eyes never left mine, and I hated what I saw when I looked into them. He was starting to see me in a different light, and that shit hurt. It was what I didn't want to happen. Not from him and especially not from Unique. Then on top of that, my mama had been blowing up my phone with calls and texts.

One of her texts said she knew what was going on and she knew I knew about Beauti being married to Rashad, it made me reject all her calls. Now, I didn't know if she knew I was a witness to the wedding because she didn't say, but I prayed she didn't. My mama was going to chew me a new asshole had she known how deep I was in this shit.

"Man, you and your sister grimy as fuck. I never thought you would do some snake-ass shit like that. Then, you refer to this girl as your sister, but didn't tell her that ol' girl was pregnant."

"Because, Ta... And please stop looking at me like that." I felt the tears forming in the pit of my eyes, causing me to take in a deep breath as I felt myself on the verge of crying.

I have never cried so much as I had since all this bullshit came out. That's why I told Beauti's ass I didn't want shit to do with it, but after begging and begging me to be a witness to her and Rashad's wedding and me constantly telling her ass no, that wasn't good enough for her. Then Rashad's dumb ass told a secret of mine that I vowed to take to my grave, and it hurt to the core that Beauti had used it to get what she wanted.

Beauti was a different kind of evil ass person. With the shit with Rashad, I found out that she would go to the extreme to get what she wanted and didn't give a damn who she hurt to get it. Finding out what kind of person she truly was, was heartbreaking to me and if I could, I would've damn sure disowned her, but we weren't raised that way.

Our parents taught us to always stick together through thick and thin. Being that I was the oldest, they were harder on me when it came to looking out for my sister, and I called myself doing just that.

"Ta, please..." I begged. "I'm already dealing with a lot. All I need from you is to be here for me. Just hug me and tell me that this nightmare would end. You know how much I talked about Nique and how much love I had for her. So you got to know how much this shit is hurting me. I never wanted to choose my sister's side when it came to them, but I had no other choice. I was in a no-win situation. What was I supposed to do?"

By now, I was crying and didn't bother wiping my tears away. I just wanted to get through to somebody. I had been sending Unique messages on Facebook since every time I called her phone, it would go straight to voicemail until I eventually stopped. She knew about Dyce because she checked my message the other day. I was hoping she would call me to talk about it, but she didn't.

A part of me wasn't even surprised. Nor could I blame her.

"Man..." Ta sang, not even attempting to console me. He basically sat beside me and watched me cry. After a while of silence, he told me, "I'm not in this bullshit, but you know Dyce is my nigga and he's fucking with Shawty hard as fuck. Me and that nigga don't talk about bullshit like this, but it's going to put us in an awkward position, too. Like, how am I supposed to go around my nigga and his woman after the one I'm fucking around with was on some disloyal ass shit like that? How can I look in Shawty's face after this bullshit, and I'm gon' have to be around her because she's fucking with my nigga?"

"So, you just don't have no faith that me and her will be friends again?" I looked at his ass like he was crazy. I mean, that was my take on what he's said. When he opened his mouth to answer me, I spoke up, adding, "And I doubt that they're going to be together. I told her all about that girl at the bar and him coming from upstairs with her."

"What?" Ta shouted, letting me know that he didn't agree with me telling Unique that. I didn't care, though, because she had the right to know. She deserved to know if anything. "Fuck you tell her that for, and not your sister being married to that nigga? And you don't even know if they were coming out of his office or not."

"Ta, ain't nobody fucking stupid. You know damn well they had been up to his office. Why else were they coming from behind the door that led up to it?" I asked, narrowing my swollen eyes at his ass. Ta knew, like I knew, what was up. No, I didn't know what they were doing, but with the way they were whispering in one another ears and then the way she said she was getting her man back, I knew something went on up there that my girl wouldn't agree on. "Nique's been fucked over by too many people, and she doesn't need Dyce fucking over her, too."

"You know what?" He asked with a chuckle as he stood to his feet, shaking his head as he looked down at me. "Just like you told me that other shit wasn't my business, that wasn't your business, either. You grimy as fuck and that shit is starting to show. You need to get your priority straight and stop running your mouth about the wrong shit. What you needed to tell her, you didn't, but wanna go run your mouth about some shit you don't even know about, hoping it would get you back in good with her? You a fucking joke and pathetic." With that, he walked off, but I was on my feet before he could make it to the door.

"I'm pathetic, really, Ta?" I screamed as I grabbed the back of his shirt to stop him from leaving. It hurt my heart that he had called me pathetic, but it hurt worse because it was true. Everything he said was true. I honestly did tell Unique because I didn't want Dyce to play her—which, in my heart, I didn't get that vibe from Dyce. He wasn't the player type, but because I wanted Unique to call and let me explain my side to her, I thought telling her about Dyce would have her reaching out to me. Now, I kind of regretted it.

"Hell, yeah, you pathetic. Now get the fuck off me!" He shrugged me off with so much force that it caused me to stumble backward, but I was right back on him, pulling at his shirt again so he wouldn't leave. I was vulnerable and didn't want to be alone.

Unique wasn't talking to me and I wasn't talking to Beauti, though I wanted to answer her calls so I could see how the twins were doing, especially my niece since she was sick. I couldn't make myself talk to her, though. Because of her, I was in their situation when I shouldn't have been. It was Rashad's fault, too, for running his damn mouth.

Had he not told my business, I wouldn't have been a fucking witness at that damn wedding or probably known about them even sleeping together. I just wanted all this bullshit to go away.

"Kels, move. Stop grabbing me… The fuck!"

"Well, stop acting like you're about to walk out on me when I just told you that I needed you here with me!" I was holding his shirt tight… so tight that the only way he could break free was if he ripped it. "Okay, I shouldn't have told Nique about Dyce, but if the shoe was on the other foot, I would want someone to tell me."

He only laughed and shook his head. There was no way I was about to tell him that he was right and the main reason I brought it up to Unique was because I wanted her to call me. I wasn't about to give his ass the satisfaction.

"I'm sorry, Ta, but please don't walk out on me. Right now, I don't have anyone. I can't even think straight. Knowing how bad Nique's hurting is killing me. I can't even rest because of all this shit and I'm scared it's going to get worse."

"Shit, I doubt it'll get crazier than this." He chuckled as he scratched his head. All the tension had gone away in his body, and I was pretty sure he would stay, but I still held his shirt. "When the fuck did they even get married?"

"A few months ago." I shook my head as I let out a heavy sigh. "But Beauti been messing with that man since before Nique got locked up. She said after she got locked up, he moved in with her. Next thing I knew, she was pregnant, and they were getting married."

"Damn, that shit is messed up."

"Yeah, it is... I told her that I didn't want to be part of it, but one thing about my sister, she is persistent. She would keep on and keep on until she got what she wanted. She always been that way."

"Is that right?" He lifted a brow as he asked that, and I knew it was a meaning behind it. When I nodded my head up and down, he asked, "Why ol' girl go to prison again?"

I released his shirt and walked over to the couch, taking a seat before I explained that Unique had taken a drug charge for Rashad. The whole time I was talking, I looked Ta in the eyes. He had an expression on his face that I didn't like. I knew what he was thinking because I had thought that myself when Unique first went to prison. I had even sat my sister down to see if she and Rashad played a part in her getting locked up, but Beauti made it clear that neither of them had anything to do with it.

She gave me some valid points on why she didn't have anything to do with Unique going to jail and the main one was, how in the hell could she have possibly known that Unique would take the charge for Rashad? That made plenty of sense to me. Unique could've easily told them who the drugs belonged to, but she didn't.

So, Like Beauti said, there was no way she could've known Unique wouldn't snitch on her man.

Running my hands through my hair, I asked Ta, "Ta, boo, could we please drop this? Like, I'm stressed. The whole situation is draining, and I no longer want to talk about it. You know everything. They were married. He's the father of her kids. I knew everything and didn't say shit. Like, there's nothing more to discuss. If you want to leave, then you can. I'll no longer stop you, but if you stay, I don't want to talk about this."

With a shake of my head, I got off the couch and headed upstairs to my bedroom, knowing if he walked out of my house, he would lock the door behind him. All I could do was pray that he didn't leave me. I didn't want him to, but if he wanted to keep questioning me about this shit, then he could go.

If I wasn't giving Unique an explanation, then I wanted to let it all go.

She was the only one that I owed anything.

Until then, I was no longer speaking about the situation. Me knowing about the marriage or the bullshit that was being held over my head that made me agree to be a witness to the wedding.

5

IN DUE TIME!

Beauti Woods-Russell

It was crazy that I had to get in my car and drive to my sister's house because she wouldn't answer the phone for me. When I saw Ta's car parked in the driveway, I rolled my eyes like any other time he was here and she wouldn't answer the phone. One thing about Kelsi Woods, she was starting to act real funny anytime his ass was around.

I didn't like that bullshit and it was making me hate his ass more and more.

Slowly getting out of my car, I walked up to her front door and knocked. It was almost ten in the morning and after feeling the hood on Ta's car; it let me know that he had stayed the night here. I was pissed.

Here I was, needing someone to drive me to the hospital to see my daughter and Kelsi hadn't been answering because she been too busy laying up.

Then Rashad, my husband, inconsiderate ass wasn't answering the phone for me, either, and he wasn't at the house he got for

Unique. I found it strange that Unique's car was there and not his, but I got out and knocked, anyway. When nobody came to the door, I felt the hood of her car. Being that it was cold; it let me know that it hadn't been moved.

It was funny to me that the stupid ass girl talked a lot of shit about beating my ass when she walked into my hospital room and assaulted me after finding out about me and Rashad, but now that I had come to the house where my husband paid all the bills at, she wouldn't even come to the door. I mean, there was no way I was going to believe she wasn't there when she had nowhere else to go. She was broke as hell and didn't have no family because her mama was dumb as fuck, just like her ass.

Unique preached all this bullshit growing up about how she would never be like her mama and be dumb over a man, only to end up just like the stupid bitch... *locked up over a man*.

Both their asses were dumb bitches, and that was the exact reason Rashad, my fucking husband, didn't marry her after they had been together for all those years.

"Kels!" I yelled as I banged on my sister's front door. There was no reason my ass needed to be over here beating on her door like I was the damn police. When I was in the hospital, fighting for my life, she promised that she would be right by my side through this, only to do the opposite. I had been calling her for a few days and not once did she return a call or respond to my text. "Kelsi... I know you're—"

The door being snatched open cut my sentence short and I was face to face with my sister. She had on a silky robe and her hair was all over her head, giving me the impression that she was doing way more than sleeping.

"Girl, why are you over here beating on my damn door like that, Beauti?"

"Because I shouldn't have to drive over here, and I just had babies."

"Well, why did you come?"

"Oh, you done started acting real funny on a bitch. Let me guess, you're mad because Nique found out about me and Shad?" I threw my hand on my hip as I waited for her to answer. My eyes narrowed as I scowled at her, waiting for her to tell me that I was right. When she didn't say anything, I rolled my eyes. "Because I was about to say, I never put a gun to your head and made you keep this a secret. Shit, I didn't even care if you would've told her. It was my husband that didn't want her to know."

"Beauti, did you come over here for that? Because I don't want to hear it. Everything is out now, so whatever."

"It is?" I gave her a look that had so much meaning behind it. "Is everything really out? Because I guarantee you there's more that can come out?"

Looking behind her, she hurriedly rushed out the door, closing it behind her. "Look, the way you keep coming at me, you can stop! It's fucked up that you're so desperate to bring me down with you. I did what you asked. I was a witness to that little wedding. Now let all the other shit go. You've done enough to the fucking girl, Beauti!"

"Oh, don't say it like I meant to hurt her, because you know I didn't Kels. I just got caught up and I couldn't help that I fell in love with him. Nique should even understand that. Isn't she violating probation just to lay up with some other man, anyway?" She huffed out an aggravating breath like she didn't want to hear what I had to say, but I didn't give a damn. Just like Unique had become my enemy, my sister was on the verge of becoming it as well, and I hated that. Kelsi and me had always had a close relationship, and I couldn't stand the fact that she was letting Unique come between our bond. "You haven't even called to check on my kids or me, knowing I'm going through all this bullshit alone."

"Beauti, Shad is your husband. He should be the one that's there for you. I've been telling you how things were going to be once Nique came home, but you were so sure that it wouldn't, and he would be in your ass. If you would've listened to me, then you wouldn't have to go through this alone."

"He's going through something right now and I'm allowing him to get himself together..." I paused, feeling myself about to cry. I knew there was no way I could tell my sister that the man that vowed to spend the rest of his life with me wanted to renege. Rashad wanting a divorce was the worst thing he would've ever said to me. My world felt like it was being ripped from me and I was going insane. I hated to be alone because of the thoughts that were constantly running through my head.

I didn't even want to live no more, thinking if I ended my life, he would hurt. I even had thoughts that if my kids were home, if I took their lives, it would hurt him the way he was constantly hurting me. I was scared and right now; I needed my sister in the worst way.

I wanted to vent to her about all this, and I had even come here to do just that, but seeing her now and the way she was speaking to me, I knew I couldn't tell her shit. I couldn't tell anyone that the reason my son had been at my parents' house since he came home was because I was scared to keep him.

"Beauti, are you fucking hearing yourself? That man hasn't been there for you or your kids since you had them. I didn't tell you because I didn't want to hurt your feelings, but when I went back to him and Nique's house and me and him got into an argument because I was telling him how fucked up it was that he left you in the hospital like that, and guess what he told me? He said that Nique needed him and told my ass to stay the fuck out of his business." She chuckled and shook her head, ignoring the tears that were now flowing down my face. "That man really looked me in my face and told me that Nique needed him after I told him you, *his wife*, was going through it. He's doing everything I warned you he would do. He's putting her before you, and that's how it's going to always be. If that baby is really his that Nique is pregnant with, you and the twins are going to come second to them. Get out of that marriage while you can, girl."

I shook my head as I wiped away my tears. My sister had never been married before, so she didn't know that in a marriage, you were supposed to accept all the pros and cons that came along with it.

Me and Rashad weren't just dating, we were married. There was no way I could just walk away from him as if this marriage weren't legal. He was mine and had vowed to love me forever. He promised to give me his all and promised to spend the rest of his life with me, and I was getting my forever. Yes, he stated that he wanted a divorce, but I knew in my heart he didn't mean it. At least that was what I wanted to believe.

We hadn't come this far only to walk away from one another, and I was woman enough to let my sister know that.

"Kelsi, this isn't a bullshit ass relationship, like the one you have with that nigga in there. Shad is my husband. My fucking husband and I'm not about to let you or nobody else come between that. I worked too fucking hard to get my happiness with him and I'm going to get it. Okay, so what he said, Nique needed him, but you know, like I know, he was only trying to be there for her because she took that charge for him. Shad doesn't want her. If he did, then I wouldn't be here rocking this wedding ring."

I held up my left hand, showing her my wedding rings I had started back wearing. It felt good that everything was out in the open and I could wear the set proudly. If only I had my husband by my side right now so we could flash them together now that he could finally start wearing his.

In due time, everything would work out in my favor.

I just knew it would.

"Or did he marry you because you told him that you were pregnant?" The fact that she had the nerve to look serious let me know she really felt that way. It pissed me off that my one and only blood sister would feel that I'm not worthy of marrying, like my husband couldn't marry me because he loved me just that much.

Kelsi was getting on my nerves with this bullshit.

"You know what? Fuck you, Kels. I knew I shouldn't have even come over here. Since Nique's dumb ass got out of prison, you have been throwing shot after shot when it comes to me and Shad, and I'm sick of this bullshit." My chest heaved up and down at a rapid pace. If I wouldn't have just given birth and was fully healed, I damn sure would've punched her ass in the mouth for talking so damn much. "I'm sick of your negativity when it comes to my marriage. What? Are you mad that he didn't ask you to marry him instead?"

"What?" she shouted, knowing damn well what I meant by that. "Look, you need to leave my gotdamn house! Clearly, you in your feelings and need to go home and sleep this shit off. If you want me to call you later when my company leaves, then I will, but I don't want to talk about this bullshit right now. As a matter of fact, I never want to talk about it again." With that, she quickly turned around and rushed inside, slamming the door in my face.

It was obvious why she had gotten offensive, but I didn't care. It was clear that Kelsi was jealous of my relationship with Rashad. She knew it and I knew it, even Rashad knew it. He was the one that had even brought it to my attention before we got married. Being that we couldn't get married without a witness, I had no other choice but to tell my sister about my relationship with him.

Automatically, she turned up her nose, asking me why in the fuck would I even sleep with that man, knowing he was with Unique. Of course, I told her it had just happened, but what her or nobody else knew was, I had always had my eyes on Rashad. Well, not always, but about four years into he and Unique's relationship, I started crushing on him.

At first, I thought it was silly and only because he was just so kind to me. Over the years, I tried to brush it off. I had even started dating the man's friend, but I quickly ended it because I felt guilty that I couldn't get Rashad off my mind. Any time I had sex with him, I thought about Rashad, and eventually; it got too much for me to handle and I stopped having sex with him. That was too much for him and he started getting it elsewhere, so our relationship ended.

Even so, I still wanted to ignore the fact that I was damn near in love with my best friend's man. Up until one night, I got the courage to go after what I wanted. I played like I was so drunk that I couldn't drive home.

I had been feeding Unique liquor all night, knowing she had never been able to hold her liquor. She was a drinker, but it would knock her ass out if she drank too much. So, knowing that, I was sure to pour her shots to the rim and make her drinks stronger than I would make mine. It was fucked up, but a bitch was on a mission.

When I knew she was good and drunk, I patted myself on the back, knowing the mission was accomplished. When Rashad finally made it home, it was game time. I was nervous as hell, but I knew it was then or never. I thought for sure he would turn my ass down. He had been with Unique for years and I knew he was faithful to her. At least I thought he was because he never gave any signs that he was a cheater, nor did Unique ever come to me about him being disloyal to her.

Her world revolved around him, and I wanted that… but I didn't want it with just anyone. I wanted it with Rashad.

The fact that he was so easy to give into me had me looking at his ass sideways that night at their apartment and he let me suck his dick. All I could think about was, that maybe he wasn't as perfect as he portrayed himself to be or as Unique thought he was, but when I was done and had swallowed his nut, the guilt that covered his face had me thinking otherwise—that maybe he was.

All he kept saying when it was over was how he had fucked up. The nigga even told me that I had to leave, but of course, I played it off like I was too drunk and didn't know what in the hell had just happened. Seeing his reaction had me feeling bad and dumb. I regretted making a pass at him out of fear that he would tell Unique.

Everything paid off, though. When he came to my apartment afterward, kicking it like he was only there to clear his name and to let me know that it couldn't happen again. I knew I had his ass right where I wanted him. I had already played drunk and put on a good-ass act like I didn't know what was going on, so there was no need for him to come to my apartment afterward, right?

It was clear that Rashad wanted me just as much as I wanted him, and now he had me. So, all that bullshit about him wanting to get a divorce was just what I'd called it; *bullshit.*

After getting in my car and driving off from Kelsi's house, I started to go to my mama's house to see my son. He had been staying over there until I was able to care for him and was no longer having crazy ass thoughts. I had just had a c-section, so I couldn't jump up and down and do for him. Now, if Rashad was home like his ass was supposed to have been, then I could've had my son home where he belonged.

My mama had offered to stay with me, but the last thing I wanted or needed was for her to be at my apartment and Rashad popped up. Yes, I had hoped that my husband would come back to me once he saw that Unique didn't want him and realized that his ass no longer had to feel guilty that she had taken that charge for him.

It was time to get over that bullshit, and I was sick of it holding me and Rashad back from being a real married couple. We had kids now, and me and the kids needed to be his only priority.

Getting out my phone as I drove home, I called my mama to see how my son was doing. She told me that he was doing fine and was taking a nap. I felt bad for having her take care of my newborn, but there was nothing I could do. Not only was I supposed to be at home recovering, but I wasn't in the right headspace to care for him right now.

His dad and sister were taking up too much of my brain to be the best mother to him, but I knew I needed to get my shit together. At least for him, I did.

"It sounds like you're in the car. Are you going to see Lovely?" My mama questioned. The past few days, my dad had been taking me back and forth to the hospital since he and my mama thought I couldn't do for myself. The whole ride would be awkward because of my situation with Rashad and the way I saw it; they should just let me be because nothing about my life was going to change.

Rashad was still going to be my husband at the end of the day, and everybody needed to accept that.

"Yeah, I'm going to see her. I went by to see Kelsi first, though." I finally responded.

My mama didn't say anything right away. She was still upset with my sister as well for being a witness at my wedding. If only she knew what I had to do in order for Kelsi to agree to it.

"Well, I was thinking about riding over there today. I haven't talked to her, and I've been calling her."

"Well, I don't want my baby over there." I made it clear. "Kels is acting real funny with me, and I don't appreciate it. To be honest, she's been acting funny since Nique came home, throwing shots at me and my man when nobody asked for her input. She was so quick to throw up in my face that Shad got Nique a house and a car, but I'm still living in an apartment. Ma, for real, I've been letting Kels slide when it comes to me and my husband, but I'm not doing that anymore. The only reason I was doing it then was because he wasn't ready for Nique to know about us. Now that everybody knows, I'm not letting nobody play with me and my marriage. Whether or not folks like it, he's still going to be my husband at the end of the day and I'm going to stick beside him."

My mama didn't say anything for a long while, and I knew she was still on the phone because I heard her background noise. There was no doubt in my mind that her silence was because she didn't like what I was saying. I didn't care, though, and as long as she was in my life, she was going to have to hear me talk about my man.

"Look, I don't agree with this bullshit, either, Beauti. I can't even wrap my mind around what in the hell you were thinking when you married that man." I got her started, and I knew she was about to read my ass. "Unique has been like a sister to you and for you to go do something like this is outrageous. I didn't raise you to betray anyone this way."

"No, you didn't raise me to betray my sister. Unique is not my sister."

"Not by blood… For years you had been calling this girl sister and now that you're had her no good ass man's baby and married that S.O.B., you want to holler she's not your sister?" She paused, I assumed waiting for me to argue with her, but I couldn't. I had just pulled up to my house and the sight of Rashad's car being parked in front of my building caused butterflies to settle in the pit of my stomach.

I wanted to end the call with my mama, but at the same time, I didn't want to seem too eager to get inside to him. That would only have me going inside my apartment and acting like a fool, ready to love on his ass when he just told me he wanted to divorce me. Despite me going against my family for him, I was still upset and very hurt that he thought he was about to leave me.

It was Unique… I knew it was her trying to get inside his head, and that was only encouraging me to go to the police station to file a report on her for assaulting me when I was in the hospital. I had witnesses, so I knew her ass could go to jail. Plus, while on probation, her ass wasn't supposed to have any dealing with the police, so it was surely going to be a win for me.

"This is wrong, Beauti, and there's no coming back from this. Even if you and Shad get a divorce, Nique would never forgive you and I honestly don't blame her. I tell you one thing, she's a better woman than me because neither you nor Shad's ass would be breathing right now." My eyes rolled as my mama snapped me from my thoughts.

I didn't say anything for a while, trying to see if she would continue talking. I had parked and was ready to get off the phone with her at this point. So, I asked, "Are you done?"

"Don't ask me no damn question like that, like you rushing me off the phone. I'm here taking care of your newborn because you can't move around like that and your so-called ass husband that you done threw away years of friendship for is nowhere to be found. Just remember one thing; what goes around, comes around. Karma is a mothafucka, and I hope nothing bad happens to you, but Karma is going to knock your ass off this high horse you're on. Just watch."

"Oh, whatever, ma." Her ass was being just like Kelsi, negative, and I didn't need that right now. Plus, she had my child, and I didn't need her taking her anger out on him. If that was the case, I would've never accepted her offer to keep him until I got better and just brought his ass home with me and my crazy ass thoughts. "I just got to the hospital to see Lovely. I'll call you later on to check on my baby. I know I won't be able to come by there today. So, if I don't call you, then I'll be by there tomorrow to see him."

She didn't even respond and just ended the call in my face. *Rude bitch.* I had never called my mama out her name before, but lately, she had damn sure been acting like a bitch. Her, Kelsi, and my dad were treating me like I had killed somebody when all I had done was hurt their precious Unique.

It was crazy because it wasn't even a guarantee that she and

Rashad would be the same happy couple everybody thought they were before she got locked up. If it wouldn't have been me, then he would've been fucking with some other bitch. Unique was gone for damn near two years. Rashad was a man. He wasn't about to go without sex for that long, especially with the way he loved fucking.

So, in my opinion, Unique's ass should've been happy that I was the one keeping his company. Hell, he could've been laid up with a nasty bitch that gave him some shit that he couldn't get rid of, and he passed it to her. However, her ungrateful ass didn't even think about that. All everybody was looking at was my friendship with her and now I was married to her man.

They didn't even act like they were upset with Rashad, and he was the one that asked me to marry him. Well, he didn't plan on it being as soon as it was. We talked about it, and he basically told me that I was going to be his wife. Then me playing around, I asked him if he was telling or asking me, and he said he was asking me to marry him.

Of course, I told him that I would and called his bluff. I told him if he was serious, then let's go to the courthouse and make it official. He was down for it, and it happened once I was able to get my sister on board. To be honest, it was the happiest day of my life. That and my kids being born, though I almost lost my damn life in the process of having them.

After unlocking my front door, I took in a deep breath before twisting the knob and opening it. My eyes closed before I walked in. It felt like I was walking on eggshells in my own shit. Rashad wasn't in the living room, confusing me because any other time he would be sitting on the couch waiting for me to get home. This time, he was in the bedroom, laying on his stomach, sleeping.

I just stood at the door, watching his back and thinking about how much I was in love with him. Words couldn't even describe how much Rashad Russell meant to me, and all I wanted was for him to get his shit together and just come home. Never in a million years did I think our lives would become this complicated.

While a part of me wanted to just let go of him and all the extra bullshit like the hurt and pain that came along with him, the other part just couldn't let go. I had waited too long for this moment, only for it to be snatched away from me.

Taking in a deep breath, I sat my purse down on the dresser and inched over to the bed where he was. God knows I wanted to still be mad at him and I even had the intention of coming in here to question him about his whereabouts, but now, seeing him made me just want to burst out with tears and beg him to come back home to me.

We've been waiting for this moment to share with the world that I belonged to him as he did me, only for him to pretend it was no longer what he wanted.

"Shad... Baby, I'm home." I leaned down and kissed the back of his head as I rubbed his back. I was sitting on the edge of the bed where he slept, and he had his head turned away from the door. Stirring in his sleep, he didn't bother to turn around to face me, so I kissed the back of his head again, trailing my kiss down to his neck, up along his jawline as I continued rubbing his back. "Baby, are you up? I missed you."

"Where you been? I been here for a fucking hour waiting for you to get here so we can go see my kids." He still had his back to me as he spoke in a calm tone.

"I went to my sister's house after I went to Unique's house, looking for you. Where have you been?" I was trying to match his calm tone, but that was impossible. I was upset and hurt, and there was no way I could hide either.

He rolled over instead of speaking, and the sight of his face caused me to leap off the bed. His eyes were black. He had a bandage on his forehead, and he was wearing a nose splint like his nose had been broken.

"What the hell happened to you?" I refused to believe Unique had done this to my man.

"Nothing." Rashad slowly sat up.

"Nothing, my ass!" Reaching out, I grabbed him by the chin and twisted his face from side to side before he knocked my hand away and told me that he was in an accident."

"What kind of accident, because your car is parked outside, and it doesn't look like you wrecked it?"

"I wasn't in my car. I was in the car I bought for Nique." I didn't know why, but I felt like my husband was lying to me. Yet, I didn't call him out on it. Unique's car was parked in the driveway when I went by there, but I couldn't remember if there was a dent or anything showing it had been wrecked. "I wanna go see my kids, though. I haven't seen them since they been born."

"Well, that's your fault that you haven't seen them, Shad. All you had to do was call me or bring your ass home."

"Nah, it ain't my fucking fault. When I went up to the hospital, yo' pops was on some other shit and got a nigga kicked out. That's why I haven't been to see them, but I'm ready to go see them now." I scratched the back of my head, not even knowing if he would be able to go back there without having the wristband. My mama had the other one, but I guess it was worth a try, especially when she hadn't been back to the hospital since Bernard had come home. "What the fuck is all that for? I can't go see my kids?"

"No, it's not that. I gave my mama the other band, but I'm pretty sure they'll still let you back there. Plus, we need to go anyway. My doctor already put in there that you're supposed to have the test done to see if you carry sickle cell traits. We need to get that done as soon as possible."

"Man, I don't understand why. I don't think I have the shit. So, she must've gotten it from you."

He had the nerve to have an attitude when he said that as he rubbed his hand down his face. With a shake of my head, I explained to him how it worked, as if I hadn't just done it the other day. "Shad, I've already told you, in order for Lovely to have sickle cell disease, both of us have to carry the trait."

"Well, have you been with some other nigga? I feel like if I had the shit, I would know."

"Son of a bitch!" I yelled as I brought my hand up to smack him only for his reflex to be so good that he grabbed my wrist before the palm of my hand could connect with his face.

"Don't fucking touch me! You see my gotdamn face is already fucked up. So, don't even try that bullshit! Fuck wrong with you?" He glared at me through narrowed eyes as I matched his stare. My chest was heaving up and down. I was so pissed the fuck off that he would even ask me some bullshit like that when he knew the twins were his. "Now, I asked you to make sure before I go take this test. I'm not trying to be surprised by shit. If I don't have this shit that you're claiming I have, I'm beating the fuck out of you, Beauti, and I'm dead ass serious about that."

I didn't even respond to him because I felt there was no reason to. I knew they were Rashad's kids and when he got his test results back and he saw everything I had been telling him was correct and they were his; I wanted an apology from his ass. I didn't tell him that, though. I was going to wait until everything came back and go from there.

In my heart, I felt after he knew for sure that the twins were his, things would be better for us. It just had to be.

"Let's go!" Snatching my arm out of his grip, I walked off. When I opened the door, Mrs. Sally was opening hers to come out as well. Behind her was a young looking chick I had never seen before.

"Hey, Beauti. How are you?" Mrs. Sally asked me. It was my first time running into her since I had to go off on her ass for telling Unique my business. In a way, I felt she had been trying to avoid me as well. I went from seeing her damn near every time I opened my door to not seeing her at all. I wasn't mad about it, though, because I damn sure didn't have time for her ninety-nine questions.

"Hey, I'm fine." My tone was dry, and I was sure not to make any eye contact with her. Not that I didn't want to, but because I was a little embarrassed for talking to her the way I did. It wasn't like she could've known I had taken him from Unique.

"That's good. How are the babies?"

"They're good. We're actually about to go to the hospital now to see our daughter. Hopefully, they'll both be home soon." She had no idea that my son was already home, and I left it as that. She was already too damn nosey and was telling too much shit.

"That's wonderful. I've been praying for them." By now, Rashad had finally locked the front door and was turning to face us. It had never taken his ass so long to lock up before, but I just assumed he didn't want to say shit to Mrs. Sally. Before all this happened, Rashad spoke to her, but he always told me that she was too damn nosey for him—which she was, but she was just so sweet that I couldn't be rude to her. However, now, I just didn't want to have any dealing with her. Cutting her eyes from my husband to me, she pushed a smile on her face and then turned to the girl that was standing beside her. "Jordyn, baby, this is Beauti. This is his wife. Beauti, this is my granddaughter."

The girl looked from Rashad to me as she flashed a smile and waved. "Hi, nice to meet you."

"Likewise," was my only response. I was upset with Rashad's ass and didn't feel like standing out here lallygagging with their asses.

"Oh..." It was written on her face that she had picked up on my attitude. "Congratulations on the babies, though, and it was nice to meet you."

As I was walking down the stairs, I didn't say anything back to her. I heard my husband finally speaking to Mrs. Sally, though, and telling her granddaughter that it was nice seeing her again. I stopped in the middle of the steps and turned around to face his ass, letting him know to cut out all that cute shit and bring his ass on.

He got the hint and started walking his ass down the stairs. *See?* Rashad wasn't ready to divorce me. He just said that shit to be funny. If he really did want to leave me, then there was no reason he would've brought his ass on down these stairs like a fucking child.

When we got inside his car and we pulled off, he asked me, "So, I take it Bernard didn't come home from the hospital yet?"

"Yeah, but he's been at my mama's house. You know I can't move around like that and then I have to go back and forth to the hospital to see Lovely. So, she suggested that he stayed with her until I got better or until Lovely came home and I didn't have to go to the hospital."

"That ain't no reason for her to keep my child." He had the fucking nerve to tell me. "You his mama, not her! His home is with you, and that's where the fuck he needs to be."

"What?" I leaned on the door to get a better look at his ass. He was being ridiculous and had some gotdamn nerve to come at me this way when he had been MIA since I gave birth to them. "Shad, I can't be jumping up and down like that. If you were home, then he would be here, and I wouldn't have to worry about nothing. I couldn't let her come to the house because there was no telling when you would decide to bring your ass home."

"Look, after we leave the hospital, we're stopping by there to get my child. So, you might as well go on and call her now and tell her to pack his things."

"If you're not going to be home, then no, I'm not calling and telling her shit. He's going to stay right where he's at." he didn't say anything as his tongue ran across his lips. His eyes remained on the road ahead and I didn't say anything, either. Lord knows I wanted to ask if he was planning on coming back home, but I didn't even want to get my feelings hurt if he said no.

Something had to give. Yes, I knew in due time things would work out and I would have the family I desired to have, but until then, Rashad had to get his shit together, because this bullshit he was on, wasn't it.

6
AT PEACE!

Dyce Walker

"So, how are things with you and ol' girl?" My brother, Tony, asked me, referring to Unique, and I knew he was because that was the only female I had brought around since my breakup with Jordyn, the last person I was in a serious relationship with.

"Okay, I guess..." I shrugged. "I mean, I guess for the most part it is."

He frowned in confusion, and I guess he had every right to be confused by my answer. "What the hell you mean, for the most part?"

"She's pregnant?" He replaced the confused expression on his face with a shocked one. Automatically, I knew what he was thinking and went on and nipped that shit in the bud. "Not by me, nigga."

"Oh, damn..." His hand shot up to his chest like he was about to have a heart attack at the thought of someone carrying my child. "I was about to say, ya'll moving a little too fast. You don't even know her like that, bro. On top of that, you said she got a nigga."

"I know her well enough." I let be known. "And she ain't even fucking with that nigga like that no more. He was on some grimy shit."

"What kind of grimy shit?"

I narrowed my eyes at him, feeling like Angie had already told him everything. I mean, they were married, and I'd always heard married mothafuckas told one another everything. I didn't know if the saying was true or not, but it was what I heard.

"Say... What kind of grimy shit?" He asked again.

"Man, I know Angie done told you the shit she had going on. Don't be playing dumb with me, nigga."

Tony threw up both hands as he shook his head. "My wife hadn't told me anything, and the only thing we ever talked about when it came to her was if we thought ya'll were serious. That's it."

I study his face for a while. I had known the nigga all my life and though he was a detective, I could tell when he was lying and when he wasn't. Right now, he was being honest with me. So, I gave him the rundown with Unique. Tony was my brother, and I knew he wouldn't tell a soul.

"Damn..." Shaking his head after I was done talking, he fell back in his seat and started drinking his beer. I did the same, minus falling back in my seat. It was a lot to take in, and only a real mothafucka would be willing to stick around and deal with it. I saw something in Unique, though, and it made me not be able to walk away from her because of her current situation. If anything, I felt she needed me. Felt like I was placed in her life for a reason.

"It's a lot, right?"

"Hell, yeah. You sure you want to deal with that bullshit? I've never known you to be in any drama, bro. You didn't even want to deal with Jordyn and her drinking and Alicia and her accusing you of cheating. This bullshit with the new girl is a lot. Are you sure you want to deal with it?"

"To be honest, I can't make myself stop fucking with her if I wanted to. She got my ass gone, man... Like, a nigga is damn near in love with her, and that shit is scary as fuck. You know, I ain't even known Shawty long, and I done bought her a ride and everything."

"What?" My brother batted his eyes like he was trying to make himself understand the crazy ass shit I had just said. All I could do was shake my head as I took a long gulp of my beer. When I brought the beer bottle down, I stood to my feet and headed to the kitchen.

After hearing myself confess that I was on the border of falling in love with Unique, I needed something stronger than beer. So, I walked over to the counter where all the liquor bottles were and grabbed the bottle of Henny, and then got a glass. I poured myself a double shot and downed it as my brother was walking into the kitchen where I was.

"Man, give me that damn bottle because after hearing you bought her a fucking car, I need a shot, my damn self." He got him a glass and poured him some, then passed it to me.

"Not just a car, nigga, but a fucking Rover!" I was saying as I passed him back the bottle and downed my drink. He shook his head and filled his glass halfway. He didn't drink it all, but after he had drunk most of the liquor, he asked me what in the fuck was I thinking. Tony was my big brother, and though I didn't always come to him about my problems, I wasn't even surprised he was about to get in my ass. "Man, I don't fucking know! Nigga, I told you, she got my ass gone..."

"Bro, she's fucking you that good for you to do some stupid ass shit like that. You barely even know that damn girl. Her pussy must be A-1."

"Aye, man... Chill out." I was all for him telling me how dumb I was, but he wasn't about to comment on Unique's pussy. Yeah, it was A-1, the best I ever had, but he didn't need to know that, and her pussy damn sure didn't have shit to do with what I had done for her. "She needed help. That mothafucka had taken her car after doing her dirty. So, hell yeah, I was looking out for her."

Tony wasn't even trying to hide his disappointment in me, and honestly, had the shoe been on the other foot, I damn sure would've been reacting the same way, minus the little shit he said about Unique's pussy. It was just some shit a mothafucka shouldn't say, and commenting on another man's woman's sex game was one. I would never do any shit like that.

"So, she's pregnant by another nigga, but got you buying her a Range Rover?"

"She ain't got me doing shit. I did it because I wanna do it."

Silence filled the air between us. I could see on his face that he wanted to say more, but there was nothing he could say about the situation to make me feel bad. As I stated before, what I did was a gamble that I was willing to take, and it wasn't like the Rover set me back in any kind of way. Honestly, I had made that little money back the next day, so it wasn't like it had put a dent in my pocket.

"So, about someone calling down to my wife's job, trying to have her arrested again... You really think it was him?" Tony asked, changing the subject. Of course, I told him all that shit and how I had gone to Shad's house about it. He let me know that wasn't smart, but I ignored him and continued telling him about the baggage that came with Unique.

"Hell, yeah. Who the fuck else it could be? The nigga knew she was out fucking with someone else and that's why he's trying to send her back to prison. It's cool though. I've already called Angie and told her that if anyone else calls about her, let me know."

"Nah, don't put my wife in ya'll drama. She doesn't need to call and tell you nothing." I frowned at his ass as I looked him up and down. He was acting like I was telling her to go out and commit a crime or some shit. All I wanted was for her to tell me if someone called up there about Unique. "I'm saying. She doesn't suppose to go back and report anything like that, especially not to you. If she's going to tell someone, it would be the sheriff's office so they could go lock her ass back up. Regardless of what my wife told her about staying out, she shouldn't be willing to risk her freedom like that."

"Damn... Really, nigga?" I couldn't even believe my brother was acting like a bitch right now.

"Yes, really." He nodded his head up and down, like what he was saying to me wasn't a big deal. I guess it wasn't to him being that he took his job serious, but at the same time, it was fucked up. "Now, by me being in the law force, what if I went and reported that since my wife clearly ain't doing her job?"

"But you're not, right?" I pushed up off the counter, standing straight up, ready to go off in his shit if he said something I didn't like.

"Of course, I'm not. For one, that would more than likely get my wife in trouble for not reporting it. I even got on to her about telling the girl that because if my wife got into any kind of trouble behind her wanting to stay out and violate probation, then there was going to be a problem."

I couldn't even find my fucking voice to go off on him. Tony was my brother, and I loved the nigga to the death of me, but he was being a straight bitch right now. I kind of wanted to beat his ass, and I knew the longer I stood here and listened to him talk, I would end up doing just that.

So, to avoid any altercation with him, I decided to just leave.

"Aye, man, I'm about to get the fuck out of here. You on some bullshit and I ain't trying to hear it. So, I'll fuck with you later." With that, I walked off with him following, telling me that I was being childish and didn't like to hear the truth. I ignored him when I really wanted to turn around and punch his ass in his mouth for talking so gotdamn much.

Inside my car, I couldn't even pull off right away. I was so upset that my ass had to calm down first. I lit a blunt and took a couple of pulls off it before I was able to drive away. I headed straight to my bar and when I got there, Unique called before I could even get out of the car.

I answered for her and when she asked what I was doing, I told her I had just pulled up at my bar. I didn't stay with her all weekend, though I wanted to. I told her that I had something to do.

All my ass did was chill at home, or when I wasn't there and at my bar, I was at Brick's house. It was funny that I didn't see Shad's bitch ass go to his house at all while I was there. That nigga was a straight-up bitch.

"Can I come to see you? I didn't see you none this weekend, and I missed you." She whined.

"You missed me, huh?" I asked, trying to play it cool, like I didn't miss her, too. "All you had to do was tell me that and I would've come to the hotel to see you."

"I know, but I just thought you wanted to be alone. I mean, the last time I saw you, you found out I was pregnant. So, I just thought you had to process that shit. I was letting you have your moment."

"You were letting me have my moment?" I repeated with a chuckle. "What made you call today, then?"

"Uh, because enough is enough." I could tell she was smiling when she said that. I let out a laugh. "I'm serious. Don't get me wrong; I know we've been sending good morning texts and whatnot, but that's not enough now. I want to see you. When I see you, I want you to tell me straight up how you feel, Dyce. I know me being pregnant by Shad and everything else I'm going through is a lot to take in, but I don't want you to hold back. I need you to always be honest with me and tell me what you think. I want to know how you feel. Not just about this, but about everything, and

I'm going to do the same. I don't want either of us holding back our feelings."

I didn't say anything for a while, and the whole time she was talking, I had my head thrown back, resting against the headrest while biting down on my bottom lip with my eyes closed, taking in everything she was saying. Honestly, I felt the same way about being open and not holding back our feelings, but this shit was different. The whole situation was, and I couldn't even put in words how I felt about her being pregnant without looking crazy.

I knew Unique had a man and there was no doubt in my mind that they were fucking, just as me and her were, but her being pregnant by him had my head fucked up. So fucked up that the last time I went to her hotel room drunk as hell was because I had turned to alcohol to cope with this shit.

Yeah, a nigga was gone off her little ass and I hated and loved it at the same time. No doubt, I wanted to be with Unique because she was someone that I saw myself building something with. I didn't give a fuck about her just coming home from prison, not having a job, or the drama that came with her. I looked past all that and the person I saw was someone I wanted to give all my love to... someone that deserved it.

Unique's life didn't have to revolve around drama. She was just in a fucked up ass position and trusted the wrong mothafuckas.

"Hello?" Her sweet tone in my ear brought me out of my thoughts, reminding me that I was still on the phone. Clearing my throat, I told her that I was still on the line. Her voice was filled with sadness as she asked, "So, let me guess, you don't want to see me?"

"Shawty, don't do that. You know I always want to see you." I voiced from the heart. "I can come to you if you want me to."

"Uh, no... I was actually thinking about going to your bar to get a Philly Cheese Steak. Ordering room service from the hotel is breaking me. In a minute, I'm not going to have enough money to pay for this room." She released a nervous chuckle. I didn't bother responding to that because had I done so, it was going to be offering her a roof over her head, and I had already bought her ass a whip. Even so, I wasn't about to have her living on the streets, though, and she had already made it clear that she didn't want to go back to the house she shared with that nigga.

The way I saw it, if she didn't want to be there, I wasn't going to let her go back. I would be a damn fool to know she didn't have nowhere else to go and not do shit about it.

"But you know I can bring you something to eat, too, right??"

"Yes, I know, but I want to get out of the room. Any chance I get to drive my Rover, I want to take it. You know I don't have friends anymore, so I've been in this room all weekend. I'm ready to get out. I'm getting out the bed now to put on some close and then I'm coming to you."

I ran my top teeth over my bottom lip as I smiled, "Come on to me then, Shawty." She giggled and said she was on the way. With that, we ended the call, and I got out and went inside.

I did as I always did—spoke to a few people as I made my way to the bar. I put in an order of a Philly cheese steak and some fries and instructed them to bring it to my office in twenty minutes, knowing it wouldn't take Unique long to get here.

Inside my office, I checked a few emails and looked over the payroll. Payday was around the corner, and I had to make sure everything was good. The good thing about this bar and grill, it was small, so there weren't that many employees. As I was looking over it, Unique called and told me that she was downstairs. I told her to walk over to my office door, but her ass was talking about ordering some food.

"Your food is up here, so hurry up and come to the door before it gets cold," I told her, standing from my desk to walk to the top of the steps to meet her. When I heard someone telling her that the door was for employees only, I told her, "Tell her you're here to see me."

"I'm here to see Dyce. He's on the phone and he told me to—"

"Oh, yeah. I remember you. You can go ahead." I knew it was Mira, the dayshift manager. She was cool as hell and fine as fuck, but she was married and let anybody she talked to know that she wasn't fucking up her happy home for nobody. That was the kind of woman I liked, and that day, she earned a lot of respect from me.

As soon as I closed my office door, I pulled Unique in for a hug. Everything with her ass felt so gotdamn natural like I had been knowing her my whole life, and I could tell she felt the same way.

"I missed you so much, Dyce." She whined, pulling back from the kiss we shared. "You know you're my big teddy bear and I can't sleep without you no more, especially during my afternoon naps."

I chuckled and shook my head as I walked out. Still, I told her, "Well, all you had to do was call. I was gon' come."

"I already told you why I didn't call you…" Walking over to my desk where the bag with her food was, she pointed at it and asked if it was hers. When I told her it was, she had the nerve to ask me how much it was. I didn't even answer her, but I gave her a look that let her know to stop asking me dumb ass questions like that.

While she sat on the couch and ate her food, I finished with the payroll. She was still eating when I got done, so I took out my phone and called up my nigga Ta. We talked until I saw that Unique was done, and I ended the call with him.

"Was it good?" I asked, already knowing it was. Not only did she demolish it, but I knew the food at my spot was top-notch.

"Delicious. Thanks so much, babe…" Standing to her feet, she walked over to me with her cup in her hand. I turned my chair as she approached me, and she wasted no time sitting on my lap. "Guess what I did today?"

I was almost scared to ask her what, but with the excitement in her voice, I knew it wasn't anything bad. "What's that?"

"I signed up for school. So, I'll be starting next Monday."

"Damn, really? That's good as fuck!"

"I know, right? I'm actually excited about it."

"I can hear it in your voice." I laughed as I cupped the side of her face, stroking along her jawline with my thumb. Her head automatically tilted, resting her face in the palm of my hand. "I'm excited for you, too, Shawty. Like, dead ass, I really am."

"Thank you." She didn't even open her eyes when she said that. There was a moment of silence as I stared at her. I wanted to kiss her so bad, but I didn't, knowing the kiss would escalate to something else. "I really did miss you, Dyce. I know it had only been two days, but I missed you so much, and it has nothing to do with your sex, either. I just missed… you."

"I missed you, too, Shawty… so fucking much," I mumbled the last part, but I was pretty sure she heard me loud and clear. Her eyes even opened as she looked at me.

"I know you were away because of this baby, Dyce, and I don't blame you because if you came to me and said you have a baby on the way, it would hurt me. I don't care if the girl was before my time or not, I would still be hurt. That's the scary thing about it because it shouldn't be that way, right? I mean, if I knew you had a girlfriend, I wouldn't have the right to be upset, would I?"

I didn't know if that was a trick question or what, but I didn't answer it. What in the fuck was I supposed to say when everything she said described me? Every emotion there was, I felt the shit right now, and it pissed me off that I still wanted to be with the damn girl, knowing if she had that bitch ass nigga's baby, I would have to kill his ass.

"The main reason I didn't call you and ask if I could see you was because I needed to process this shit, too. Since me and Shad became serious with one another, all I ever dreamed about was to have that nigga's baby... to wear his last name. Although I've cried and asked God why I was going through this, I had to laugh... I'm talking, I really laughed like I never had before. All weekend, I laughed to the point where I was crying. Your words kept replaying in my head, to boss up on that mothafucka. Now, I'm still going to beat Beauti's ass every time I see her, but I'm going to get my shit together and do as you said. In order to do that, I had to make a doctor's appointment this morning."

I raised a brow as she paused. I saw so much life in her eyes at the moment, almost like she was proud of herself and was finally over the bullshit.

"Tomorrow, I just need a couple of hours of your time... I've never gotten an abortion before, so I don't know how I'll feel afterward. When I made the appointment, she asked if I would have someone driving me and I told her I would. The only person I have is you."

I dropped my head.

Though I didn't want her to be pregnant by that nigga, I didn't know how to feel about her getting an abortion, either. I just didn't want her to do something like that because of me, especially with her just saying how she had always dreamed of having his baby. The last thing I wanted was to come in and intervene on that.

"If you don't want to, then I can always catch an Uber."

"It ain't that I don't want to, Shawty... It's just..."

"What?" She leaned down and gave me a peck on the lips. It was so out of the blue as if she had been waiting her whole life to do that. "What is it then?"

"Are you sure you wanna do that? I mean, that baby is a part of you, and I don't want you to do no shit like that because you're worried about how I'll feel. As bad as I hate to admit it, I don't even think a baby with that nigga will make me stop fucking with you."

While I felt like a dumb ass for saying that stupid ass shit, she looked surprised, like she couldn't believe it. Hell, I couldn't even believe I had just stated those words aloud. What I did know was; it was the fucking truth.

Finally, after a long sigh, Unique stared me dead in the eyes and told me, "I really appreciate that, Dyce. Those words were everything, and although I've always known you were a good man, you've just proven to me that you're truly one of a kind. You know how Rashad is, and me having his child would only make the situation worse, you still willing to be here means so much." She leaned down and pecked my lips again as she brought her hands to the side of my face. When she pulled back, she was still cupping my face as she stared into my eyes. "That shows a lot about your character, but baby, I would never put you in that position. I don't even want to be in that position. I don't want nothing that is attached to him and that's why I'm getting this abortion. It has nothing to do with you, so I don't even want you thinking about that. I mean, yes, I've thought about your feelings since I found out I was pregnant, but it's not why I'm going through with it. I'm at peace with this. It's something I want to do and something that I am going to do. Okay?"

I ran my tongue over my lips as I nodded my head up and down. No lie, it felt good as hell to hear her say that, and for that, since she was at peace with it, I was damn sure taking her to handle her business.

7
NEVER KNEW!

Rashad Russell

I had been sitting at the edge of the bed for all of ten minutes, trying to wrap my mind around the call I had just received. It was from the doctor, and it had my ass stuck. I guess I should've been happy with the news, but I wasn't. It was too much shit to process, and before I took the shit to anyone else, I had to get a clear understanding of it first.

"Man, what the fuck?" I mumbled to myself as my head shook. I knew I had to get my ass up because sitting here replaying the conversation in my head as if it would somehow change wasn't doing shit but fucking my head up worse than it already was.

Grabbing some more of the bags I had packed while here, I headed back outside to my car. I was moving my clothes out of the house before I called Unique to tell her that I was moved out and was giving her the house. I had made up my mind to continue paying the rent and all the bills until she was able to get on her feet. I guess I owed her that much.

I was giving her back the car and everything. My only request was going to be for her not to bring that bitch ass nigga in my shit, though. It fucked me up that I didn't even know where she lived and if I knew where he stayed, I would ride past his house just to see if I saw her outside.

I had even gone to the probation office to see if I could catch her going in or out, but she hadn't been there, either. She was violating in a major way. Being that she wasn't locked up, it made me wonder if she was on the run because her ass was supposed to have been back behind bars. Then again, her probation officer wasn't even doing her damn job.

As I walked out my front door, I looked up the street to see if that fat ass nigga was up there. I didn't see his car, but I saw Ta's and after putting my bag in the trunk; I walked to the end of the driveway and called his name. It was only three niggas standing out, so he wasn't hard to spot. When he turned to face my direction, I waved my hand so he could know it was me that had called him.

He started walking my way, and I met him halfway.

My face had started healing and I no longer wore the shit on my nose that the doctor told me that I needed to wear for three weeks. I refused to continue walking around looking like a fool. I had already lied to my wife and told her that I was in a car wreck. Because of that, I had to pull Unique's car into the garage in case she tried to do her own investigation—which, she had no reason not to believe me.

My parents were the only ones that knew what really happened.

"Aye man, what's up?" Ta spoke when he approached me. We dapped one another up as we always did.

"Shit. Tell me why yo' boy came to my house the other day. I don't know if he broke in or what, but when I got here, he was sitting in my shit, drinking my last beer and shit like his..." I caught myself. Me and Ta were cool and everything, but I knew how close him and Dyce were and I wasn't trying to start no shit by calling his boy a fat ass or stating how black his ass was. I couldn't say enough how much I hated his ass. "I mean... Like the nigga was at home."

"Oh, yeah... I thought you were about to say some fly shit." Ta gave me a death stare. *See?* I knew I couldn't call Dyce's bitch ass out of his name. He had mothafuckas ready to defend his ass like he was God or somebody. "But what about it?"

I ran my hand down my face, growing impatient with his ass. It had never been any beef between me and Ta, but I guess because he was loyal to Dyce, he wanted to act like we were never cool.

"I was just saying, but... Fuck it!" I didn't even want to talk to him about the shit, because it was obvious that he knew about it, talking about, *what about* it? The nigga might've been the one that was driving his car by my house to throw me off. Just the thought of it had me pissed, but I tried not to let it show, being that I had a question that I was hoping he could give me the answer to. "Have you seen Nique? I know you fuck with Kelsi, so I'm trying to see if she at least reached out to her or something.

"Nigga, are you really sitting here asking me about that damn girl after you married her homegirl?" I just stared at him, not even bothering to answer his question. I guess I shouldn't have been surprised that he knew what was going on being that he was fucking with Kelsi, but I couldn't even fake like the shit didn't make me angry that she had been, clearly, pillow talking to the nigga about my business. On top of that; there was no telling what all he knew and how she had twisted everything to make me look like the bad guy. "Man, don't even ask me shit about that girl."

"Look, man. We never had beef or no shit like that and I'm not trying to have none now. All I want to know is—"

"And it still ain't no beef with us." He cut me off. "I just ain't about to answer no damn questions about her. I don't know Shawty like that, but it's fucked up how you did her. If you wanna know something about her, then you find the shit out yourself, but don't ask me shit." With that, he turned around and walked off, leaving me standing here pissed the fuck off.

It didn't take a rocket scientist to know that he was only acting this way because of Dyce. Had Unique not been fucking with his homeboy, Ta wouldn't have given a damn one way or the other about how I had done her. So, all that fake concern bullshit, he could've kept to his gotdamn self, because I saw right through it.

Shaking my head, I turned around and headed back to the house to get the last of my things to take to my mama's house. Beauti didn't even know I was moving out of this house, and I wasn't telling her. She had already been asking me what I was going to do with the house when I told her that Unique had left me.

I knew if I told her my plans for the house, to let Unique keep it, it would've started a battle that I wasn't trying to fight with her ass, especially when she still wanted us to get a house together. That was a no. I didn't even want to be in this marriage with her ass no more because I wanted to make things right with Unique and I knew I couldn't do that and still be Beauti's husband.

At the same time, I had been stalling going up to the courthouse to file for the divorce because I knew how bad it would hurt her. Yes, I still loved her that much to care about her pain... She was the mother of my kids, so I didn't want to cause her any pain, but I knew it had to have been done sooner or later. I felt the appropriate time was when my daughter came home. That way, she wouldn't have to stress about the divorce *and* our daughter.

Once I had everything I was taking to my mama's house, I got in my car and headed that way. I pulled up and got out. Though I had been staying at Beauti's house, my mama knew I was bringing my clothes here and letting Unique get the house. Despite me telling her that Unique had the nigga she was fucking with to come into the house and beat my ass, my mama still felt I was doing the right thing.

Her biggest argument was that Unique didn't have a family and, as a man who had both his parents and could come back home at any given time, she deserved the house. It was the truth, though, especially with how I had done her, so there was no argument from me. *See?* My mama loved herself some Unique, and that was the main reason I couldn't tell her I had gotten her best friend pregnant and married her.

"Hey, you need help?" My mama asked me in a whisper as she covered the mouth part of the phone with her hand. I shook my head and walked back out the door to get the second bag. In all, it was three large black bags full of clothes and shoes, amongst other things I felt I needed. The few other things I left behind were staying, in case Unique decided to move back into the house, it would be something of mind still left there.

All the pictures of us were still there, minus one that I had brought with me and sat on my nightstand. Though I was barely here, I wanted to have something to look at when I did come. Sure, my mama had pictures of us around the house, but I wanted to come lay in bed and have time to myself to reminisce on all the good times we shared.

After I had everything in the room, I didn't bother putting anything up and just placed the bags inside the closet. I already had clothes at Beauti's house, so there was no need for me to take any of my bags there. Plus, the damn apartment was already small and with the twins' shit, there was no more space for me to bring anything else in there.

"Hey, you good?" My mama tapped on the room door where I was, walking from inside the closet. When I turned to face her, she was peeking her head in.

"Yeah, I'm good," I told her. Actually, I was glad she had come up to check on me because I wanted to talk to her about the news I had received today. I was still trying to process it, but before I went to Beauti or Unique, I had to let my mama know about my results from the test. "Okay, I was just checking on you. Have you talked to Nique? I've been leaving her messages on Facebook to call me so I can see what in the hell is going on, but she hadn't called yet. I don't like this, Shad, and I feel like it's something that you're not telling me. If Nique is talking to someone else, it has to be a reason for her—"

My face contorted into a frown as I cut her off. "So, you're blaming me for her being with some other nigga?" I shouldn't have even been surprised.

"No, I'm not blaming you, but I'm just saying..." She paused, letting out a heavy sigh. "Something isn't adding up Nique loves you, and everybody that knows ya'll knows just how much. So, for her to be with another man after all the years ya'll shared together, something's not right."

I just stared at my mama. I wanted to tell her the reason Unique ended up fucking with someone else, but I just couldn't bring myself to tell her I was the one that pushed her right into the arms of another man. Then I would have to tell her about my marriage and my kids, and a nigga wasn't ready for all that yet. No, I wasn't ashamed of my babies, or Beauti, but it was just the situation, and I knew not only my mama but my dad wouldn't be pleased with this shit.

Somewhat changing the subject, I ran my hand over my face as I huffed out a deep breath while taking a seat at the foot of my bed. My back was to the door as I started speaking. "I went to the doctor the other day, and they did blood work on me. I got a call back right before I came here and it turns out, I carry sickle cell traits. I don't even know what that is, and I damn sure didn't know I had it."

"Have you been sick and hadn't told me?" My mama's voice was laced with much concern when she asked me that. She even walked over to the bed where I was and stood in front of me. When I looked up at her, her eyes were bucked, and she looked like she was on the verge of tearing up. "You should've told me if you have been, Rashad."

"Nah, ma..." I threw up a hand, letting her know that I was okay and there was no need for her to be dramatic. "I hadn't been sick at all."

"So, you just went to the doctor for a checkup, and they tested you for that?"

I dropped my head and didn't say anything, trying to think of a story to tell her besides the real reason I had a test done. I had already lied and told her I went to the doctor, instead of letting her know I had the test done at the hospital. Again, I would then have to tell her the truth.

"I guess they just gave the shit to me, but now I have to find a way to get in contact with Nique because she is pregnant?"

"What?" my mama shouted. "Rashad, why didn't you tell me?"

"Tell you for what? I mean, eventually, I was going to tell you, but I've just been dealing with a lot." She dropped her head, shook it, and mumbled something. I was surprised because since it was Unique that was pregnant by me, I thought her reaction would've been a lot different from the one she was showing. "Hold up, you're mad that Nique is pregnant?" I wanted to know.

"No, I'm not mad that Nique is pregnant. What kind of question is that?" She had the nerve to look at me like I was the one that was overreacting right now. "It's just, I wish you would've told me, then I could've been the one that let you know of your sickness."

"What?" My eyes batted a few times as I shook my head, knowing I didn't hear her right. The fuck she meant, *tell me about my sickness*? Of course, I knew what it meant, but I refused to believe my whole life I had this shit, and my mama hadn't told me.

"Shad, baby... You were born with sickle cell traits. I carried it and passed it on to you."

"What?" I jumped up, pissed the fuck off that she didn't tell me about this shit before now. "What you mean you passed it on to me? So, all my life you knew I had this but didn't tell me."

"Because, baby, it's not life-threatening. It never affected me, and I was told that more than likely, it wouldn't affect you. When you were younger, the doctors kept a close eye on you to make sure everything was okay, and you would live a healthy normal life. You are, and I didn't see a reason to tell you. I mean, eventually, I knew I was going to have to when you decided to have kids, but—"

"When I decided to have kids? So, you were going to wait until someone got pregnant by me like you did?"

"No... Well, actually, I didn't think you and Nique would have kids now. She always talked about marrying you and then having kids. So, I was waiting until the right time."

"The right time would've been when I was old enough to understand." I shook my head. "That's messed up, Ma. You should've been told me. Now I have to hunt this girl down and tell her about this shit, and I heard that if two people carried the trait, then the baby could come out with sickle cell disease. I don't even know if Nique got it or what. So, she needs to be tested."

I hadn't done no research whatsoever and was just going by what Beauti said.

"And that's true." My mama nodded her head up and down, staring at me through apologetic eyes. "That's how you ended up carrying the trait because your dad doesn't show any signs of the trait or the disease."

"Man..." I dragged out the words, pissed to the core. Had I even known all this shit, I didn't even know if I would've even had kids, or if I did, I would've been sure to tell any woman that I planned to have them with about it. Now, my daughter was sick, though

Beauti carried it, too, and didn't know, there was a possibility that the child Unique was carrying would be born with it, as well.

At least if Unique didn't carry it, the baby would probably carry the trait and not the disease like Lovely. Lord knows a nigga wasn't trying to have two babies with the same illness.

"Shad, baby, I'm sorry. I should've told you, but I'll try to keep getting in touch with Nique so I can tell her to get tested and we all go from there. In the meantime, you do the same. I mean, if she's pregnant with your child, then there's no way she could avoid you forever. So, just keep calling her and leave her messages if you have to, and if I talk to her before you, then I'll call you and let you know."

I couldn't even say shit. I was so upset that all I wanted to do was leave the house. The sight of my mama only made me madder. There was no reason she should've kept something as serious as this away from me. This wasn't just the flu or no shit like that. It was something that was genetic. Something she should've sat me down and talked to me about.

After leaving the house and letting her apology go in one ear and out the other, I went to the liquor store and got myself two six-packs of bud ice, then headed to me and Beauti's apartment. When I pulled into the parking space and got out, I saw that I was parked next to Jordyn's car. I didn't know she was sitting inside until I got out and was heading up to the building.

"Hey, congratulations on the babies again." Her sweet voice caused me to stop in my tracks and turn back around to face her. I was glad that my face was healing up. Being that my skin was on the light side, I still had marks underneath my eyes from my nose being broken, and I couldn't wait until that shit was gone.

The last thing I wanted was for mothafuckas to think I'd gotten my ass beat—which if anybody asked, I was sticking to the lie I had told my wife; I was in a car accident.

"Aye, what's up?" I pushed a smile on my face as I turned

around and walked the short distance to her car. She was smiling from ear to ear as she, once again, gave me the fuck me eyes like she did the first time I met her. "What you doing sitting out here in the car?"

"I was getting ready to leave, but I wanted to make a phone call first to see if I was going back to my hotel or if I could make other plans instead."

Without my consent, my tongue brushed around my lips as I lifted a brow. "Damn, I wish I could be the other plan you're making."

She licked her lips before pressing them together, blushing as she asked me, "And what would your wife have to say about that?"

From that alone, I knew she would be down to fuck. "What she doesn't know won't hurt her."

Laughing, she told me, "I hear you. So, you're that type of man, huh? The type that doesn't take his vows serious."

"Nah, I take them serious. I ain't no cheater or nothing like that, but with yo' fine ass, I'm willing to take it there."

"Really? Because I'm fine as hell; you're willing to cheat this one time? That ain't right." I couldn't even say shit, because she was right... No matter how fine she was, it shouldn't have been a reason to make me step out on my marriage. Over the years, it had only been Unique and Beauti for me. I didn't want another woman because I didn't need one. However, right now, at this point in my life, it was whatever.

This marriage wasn't even what it used to be.

I loved Beauti, but my heart wasn't in it as it was about a month ago.

"How about I give you my number and we see if we could make that happen?" I was shocked to hear those words leave Jordyn's mouth. Showing all thirty-two teeth, I turned around to my window to see if Beauti was looking out. I couldn't even tell, but I didn't want to risk her seeing me pull out my phone and program Jordyn's number in it. So, I told her to just take mine. She immediately grabbed her phone, and I called it out to her. When she had it saved, she told me, "Now, you make sure wifey doesn't get your phone when I call you."

"Oh, you good. Just text me first and if she's not around, then I'll call you and we can set something up." I was trying to fuck. Point blank. "As a matter of fact, call my phone now so I can have your number. I'm texting yo' fine ass tonight."

Giggling, she hit send on her phone, and not even two seconds later; I felt my phone vibrating in my pocket. After telling her that I would hit her up tonight, she told me that she looked forward to talking to me and I walked off. Before I even made it up to the building, she was backing out of the parking space and pulling off.

When I reached the top step, Mrs. Sally was walking out with her broom. It was like she waited until I walked up to come out. She was so damn nosey that it didn't even surprise me that she knew I was talking to her granddaughter. She told me in a hushed tone, "Stay away from my grandbaby before I tell your wife what I just saw."

"What?" I scowled at her old nosey ass. "Man, stay the hell out of my business!"

Instead of sweeping, she went back into her house and slammed the door, leaving me standing in front of mine, shaking my head.

Her old ass needs a gotdamn man! I thought, as I took my key out of my pocket and opened the door. I didn't see Beauti, but I sat my beer on the counter and walked over to the bassinet to see that my son was lying inside sleeping. I pushed a one-sided smile on my face then walked off to put my beer in the refrigerator and get myself one.

I popped the top on the can and then headed to the back of the house. The bathroom door in our bedroom was opened, and I heard the water running. I walked into Beauti in the shower. I breathed a sigh of release because that meant she didn't witness me and Jordyn exchange numbers.

I snatched the shower curtain back, causing her to nearly jump out of her skin and try to cover her naked body. When she saw it was me, she told me that I had scared her and asked when I got home. Instead of answering her, I looked her body up and down and told her, "Damn, those kids got that ass fat."

I was horny and wanted some pussy in the worst way. She had been sucking my dick, but I was sick of that. I wanted to feel her insides. That was another reason I wanted to hit Jordyn up tonight. I wanted some pussy from her since I couldn't get it from my wife yet.

"I know, right? I was looking at that earlier." She was blushing hard as hell. "You want to get in with me? We hadn't showered together in a long time, and I missed that."

"Nah, because if I get in there, I'ma be tryna fuck and you can't do that yet."

"But there are other things we can do." I figured she was talking about sucking my dick and I didn't want that. Don't get me wrong; Beauti knew what she was doing when she had my dick in her mouth, but I wanted some pussy. I wanted the head of my dick to hit the bottom of her stomach. "Oooh, and you know what else we hadn't done in a while?"

"What's that?" I took a long gulp of my beer as I awaited her answer.

"Anal... We can do that if you want to." I pushed my bottom lip into my mouth, contemplating taking her up on her offer. I opened my mouth to tell her that it was okay because I really wasn't trying to hurt her, being that she had just had the, but she spoke up. "Honestly, I feel like if we go slow, we can still have sex. I'm not even hurting no more."

"Nah, man. You just had the kids. You need to heal. I'm good." With that, I turned around and walked back. Out the bathroom, going into the living room. I could see in her eyes that she was only willing to have sex because she was afraid if she didn't give it to me, I would get it elsewhere.

It made a nigga feel bad because that was exactly what I had plans to do.

Sitting my beer on the table, I got my phone out of my pocket and called Unique only for the call to go straight to voicemail—which it had been doing for a few days. I knew she had my ass on call block, and I couldn't leave her no messages on Facebook because she had a nigga blocked on there as well.

This is some straight up bullshit. I thought as I grabbed my son out of his bassinet. I couldn't wait until my daughter came home. They had to first get her breathing under control. Not only did my baby girl have sickle cell disease, but according to the doctor, she had a bad case of asthma, too. I felt so bad and wondered if all this shit was happening to her because of how me and Beauti had done Unique.

As much as I asked myself if it was because of that, I refused to believe it was, being that our son was in good health. The way I saw it, if that was the case, then both of them would be sick. *Right*?

"What's up, man?" I kissed my son on the cheek. I couldn't believe I had kids and with someone other than Unique, too. When she was locked up, I tried not to think about her not being the one to carry my firstborn, but it was always in the back of my head. Even when I thought I was over her, that thought wouldn't go away.

Staring down at my son, I tried to see my feature in him, but I couldn't. He didn't look like Beauti, either, and I guess it was because he was a newborn, and his looks hadn't come through yet. I knew he was mine, though. The only reason that he and his sister not being my kids even crossed my mind was because of his sister's illness. Now, after the doctor explained to me the same thing Beauti did about what we were diagnosed with, I knew for sure they were mine and didn't feel the need to get a paternity test.

Still, I didn't understand why Bernard wasn't sick, no matter how much they told me it was because they were born in two different sacs. That shit was odd to me.

"Awww... Let me take ya'll picture, bae." Beauti said then disappeared back out of the room. When she returned, she had her phone in her hand and was grinning from ear to ear, loving this moment. A couple of months ago, I would've loved it, too, but right now, everything seemed forced to me. Even so, I put on a good act as if I was still happy about our situation.

After the many pictures of me and my son and even a few with the three of us, Beauti started posting them on Facebook without my permission. I wanted to tell her to delete them, but I knew she would have a fucking fit if I told her that, especially since everything was out in the open.

I knew she had deleted Unique, though, because she told me that she did. So, I guess I shouldn't have been worried about it.

She read the caption aloud as she posted the picture, messy ass. *Me, hubby, and son waiting for our Lovely to come home.* She smiled from ear to ear when she posted it and showed it to me. It was the first picture of us since we made everything official.

"Here, put him back in the bassinet for me. I wanna talk to you right quick." I instructed.

"About what, Shad?" Instead of doing what I asked, she remained sitting and looked at me with a hard scowl.

"Man, just put him back in the damn thing." This time, she sucked her teeth and grabbed Bernard to do as I asked. She tried sitting on my lap after she put him in his bassinet, but I told her not right now.

"Please don't tell me you about to start back up with this damn divorce bullshit, Shad, because I don't want to—"

"I got a call from the doctor before I came here..." I voiced, shutting her up. The frown on her face vanished.

"And?" she said.

"Fuck you mean, and... You were right about everything. I carry the trait, too." She started yelling about how she tried to tell me, but I wasn't in the mood for that shit. "Okay, damn! I talked to my mama about it, and she knew. I wish I would've gone to her and told her that you were pregnant, so I could've already been prepared for this shit, or we could've just terminated the pregnancy too—"

"No, the fuck we couldn't! Shad, don't damn play with me!" She looked like she was ready to slap my ass for uttering something like that. It was fucked up, and I was sure to apologize for it. "You should be sorry. That shouldn't have even crossed your damn mind. Are you planning on telling Unique to abort that baby, or you already know it's not yours since she's fucking somebody else?"

"Aye, don't start that shit," I warned in a serious tone with a look to match. "Nique ain't pregnant by no other mothafucka. So don't even let that fly shit come out your mouth again. As a matter of fact, this ain't about Nique. It's about us, and Lovely, and where we go from now."

"We're going to keep on living as we've been living. This shit hadn't even affected us and we're not going to let it." Her tone was calm as she stood and then sat on my lap. I allowed her. As much as I hated it and though it didn't seem I did, I still had a lot of love for Beauti. She knew it, too. "Our daughter is going to be okay, too. I talked to the nurse, and she told me that she's improving more and more as the days go by. So, she's expected to be home soon."

"That's what's up right there." I pushed a smile onto my face. No lie; that was music to my ears. "I can't wait for my baby girl to get here, and I was thinking, since you and Nique ain't together no more, we should just move into the house instead of trying to find another one. There's no need for you to give up that house when it's big enough for us."

My body stiffened when she said that. It wasn't even possible for me to agree to that when I wanted Unique to move back in there.

Although I knew the apartment was too small for Beauti and our kids, she was just going to have to tough it out, because moving into the house I still had hopes me and Unique could grow old in, just wasn't happening.

Instead of flat-out telling her no, I told her that I would think about it and then kissed her lips before she could say anything else.

8
YOU PUT A SPELL ON ME!

Unique James

Besides the first day I reported, I had never really breathed a sigh of relief after walking out of my probation office because I never had a reason to, but this time, with all that was going on in my life and someone, who I assumed to be Rashad, calling and trying to report me for staying out longer than my curfew, I was so relieved that I was able to walk out and didn't get locked up.

Mrs. Walker had been so understanding that with everything that was going on in my life, she let me skip coming in to report and just call instead. I had missed two Wednesdays straight, and I wasn't about to make it a third one. The last thing I wanted was to get too comfortable and people start to notice I hadn't been coming in.

She assured me the other day when she called to check on me that I was okay and that I could use the time to get myself together. I let her know everything was good. Dyce had been staying at the hotel with me and had even paid for me to stay there for another month—which, I told him he didn't have to. Honestly, I was glad he did because although I was trying to be independent, I really needed him in the worst way.

I only had enough money on my cash app that would cover one more week, so he had truly come through for me. Without him, I didn't know what I would do.

After getting inside my car, I texted Dyce to let him know I was leaving the probation office and heading back to the hotel room. Of course, he was the one that had suggested I called him when I left, but I decided to send him a text instead. He texted right back, telling me that he would see me soon.

With that, I started up my engine and headed to my next destination. When I pulled up to the house and parked on the side of the road, I didn't bother getting out right away, though the person knew I was coming. I had made it clear that I couldn't stay long because for one; I didn't want Dyce to beat me to the hotel and two, the last thing I wanted was for Rashad to come to his parent's house and I was here.

Rasheeda had been sending me messages after messages on Facebook and calling my phone. I wanted to block her like I'd done to her son, but I had to think, there was no way she could've known what was going on, just like I didn't think Beauti's parents knew.

Those might've been her parents, but they didn't play that bullshit. Unlike Kelsi, who clearly knew what was going on, Mama B and Papa P were all for doing the right thing. I felt bad that I wasn't answering Mama B's phone calls or responding to any of her messages that she was sending, telling me that she wanted to talk to me. She was even apologizing for what her daughter had done to me and swore up and down that she didn't know,

My heart knew she didn't, but I just needed time to mentally and emotionally heal before I sat down and talked to her.

Finally getting out after having Rasheeda standing on the

porch waiting long enough, I walked up to where she was, and she smiled as she took my hand and pulled me into the house.

"You want anything to eat or drink?" She asked me and I declined. I had just grabbed myself something to eat on the way to see Mrs. Walker, so I was still kind of full from the Burger King I'd gotten. "Okay... Uh, what is going on, Nique? All Shad has been telling me is that you're seeing someone else, and the man you're seeing broke into his house and attacked him. He said you had him do that."

"What?" I shouted. "I've never had anyone attack Shad, and I doubt he was even attacked."

"Yeah, I had a hard time believing you would have someone do that, too, but someone did attack him. He had to go to the hospital about his nose and everything."

"Oh, I know he got beat up. He sent me the pictures and called me accusing me of sending someone over there, but what I mean by I doubt he got attacked is, I'm pretty sure he just got beat up... Like, he lost a fight."

Rasheeda didn't bother retorting anything in response, and I guess I didn't blame her. At the end of the day, Rashad was her son, and I knew she didn't want to think about another man beating his ass.

"Well, are you guys still together?" I could tell by the expression that washed over her face that she hated she asked that question as soon as it rolled off her tongue. She shifted in her seat as she cleared her throat. "Well, I guess ya'll aren't if you're seeing someone else. What happened? Like I told Shad, I know it had to have been something he did on his end, because of how much you loved him. You never hid that, so for you to be with someone else, he had to have done something."

I didn't answer her right away because I didn't feel it was my place to tell her the bullshit Rashad had been on. Not only that, but I was trying not to make him look bad. That feeling didn't last long, though. As soon as I started thinking about how nobody considered my feelings and how it would make me look, I went on and told her everything.

I said, "Rashad got a set of twins that were born not too long ago." The seriousness on my face let her know I wasn't lying, and Rasheeda knew me and knew I wouldn't even joke around about something as serious as that. "Not only that, but Beauti is his *wife* and the mother of his twins," I emphasized wife and that caused her bottom lip to damn near hit the floor.

"What? He's married?" She leaped up from her seat, throwing her hand on her hip. "And ain't that bitch your friend?"

"She *was* my best friend... Apparently, her and your son were sleeping together before I got locked up and after I was sent to prison, they got married. He claimed he only married her because she got pregnant, but I don't want to hear that shit. He married her because he was clearly in love with her."

"Whoa... Wait a minute." She shook her head as she took a seat, closing her eyes to process this shit. It was a lot, and I knew it was hard for her to believe it, just as it would've been for me had I not seen the shit with my own eyes. "How do you know this, Nique? I'm not saying you're lying, but are you sure?"

"I saw it... I got word that her husband took her to the hospital and I went up there."

"But how did you know it was him? Did someone tell you it was him?"

I took in a deep breath and explained to her how Shad had been treating me since I came home, staying out all night and coming home late at night. I even explained how Beauti had been pulling back from our friendship like she secretly had animosity toward me. At the time, I didn't know she really did, though.

"It was just something off to me, but I still didn't want to believe my best friend and my man were messing around and they had been bold enough to come to the prison to pick me up together."

"Wow... Sneaky mothafuckas."

"Exactly." I agreed with Rasheeda with a chuckle. "But on the drive to the hospital, I started thinking about all that and when I got there, something just didn't seem right to me, but I still didn't want to think *that*. Yet and still, I walked up to the front desk and asked if they had a Beauti Woods and the lady told me, no, so I explained how she had recently gotten married and gave her Shad's last name. When she said she had a Beauti Woods-Russell, that confirmed everything. A part of me still wanted to believe they wouldn't do me like that, but when I saw her name tag on the door and then walked in the room to him right by her side, I knew it was true."

"I would've dragged that bitch out of that fucking bed and killed Shad's ass, right then and there." Rasheeda was pissed and wasn't trying to hide it. "What in the hell were they thinking? I'm about to call his ass!" She got up and headed out the living room, ignoring me telling her not to call Rashad until I left.

I didn't even want to see his face right now. Getting up, I rushed into the kitchen where she was, and she had her phone in her hand.

"Please, I'm begging you, don't call him while I'm here."

"Why not? He's not going to do anything to you for telling me this. I'm glad you told me."

"I'm not worried about that. I just don't want to see him."

"Why? Because you're pregnant?" Rasheeda questioned. "So, the negro could tell me that you're pregnant by him, but couldn't tell me he had twins. I knew she was pregnant, but Shad being the father was the last thing I would've thought."

"Because he knew it was wrong... Him and Beauti, both." I chuckled, though it felt like someone was twisting the knife in my back deeper and deeper the more I talked about it. Even so, I added, "Shad's not dumb. He knew you wouldn't be okay with this."

"You damn right I'm not and neither will his dad. I can't wait until I get home and tell him... As a matter of fact..." She grabbed her phone off the counter. "I'm about to call him now and tell him, and you know what, Nique, it explains where his ass been. Since your boyfriend or whoever broke into the house, he stayed over here a couple of nights and then started staying somewhere else. I asked him where, but he tried to tell me at the house in case you come back. I told his dad he was lying. I just felt like he was, but the other day, he brought his clothes and shit here and said he was letting you get the house. I didn't even bother going through the bags because I thought they were his things, now I'm wondering if there were yours and he's going to move her and those kids in the house."

"What? You really think he brought my stuff here?"

"Girl, I don't put shit past Shad's ass now. I'm so pissed off I'm shaking."

"Where did he put the stuff at?" If it was my clothes, I wanted them. I had gone to Walmart to get myself some leggings and a couple of T-shirts because I was running out of clothes and wasn't trying to spend any extra money on any. I got a few bras and underwear, but I was running low on those, too. I hid all that from Dyce because I didn't want him trying to buy me anything to put on. Accepting money to buy me clothes was weird, I already felt like a charity case.

I mean, I wouldn't mind asking Rashad, being that I had been with him for ten years, but Dyce was a different story. I hadn't known him long, and he had already done enough for me.

"They're upstairs in the closet. You can go look up there if you want. I'm letting you know now, I'ma be pissed the hell off if he's up to some bullshit like that. I don't care if she does have his kids or the fact that they're supposed to be married. He got that house for you and he's not letting some other bitch move in there."

I didn't even bother responding to her because I didn't care one way or the other if Rashad moved his family into that house. I just wanted the clothes that he bought me. The last thing I wanted was to see the bitch rocking my shit.

Walking out of the kitchen, I headed upstairs to Rashad's old room. Before I could get up the stairs good, I heard Rasheeda on the phone, fussing to her husband about the news she had just found out. I walked into the room and looked around as if it was my first time being in it. The bed was a mess and on the nightstand was a picture of me and Rashad. I picked it up and stared at it for a while, remembering the exact day we took the picture. It was one year we had gone to the fair. Beauti and his friend that she was seeing had gone as well.

Chuckling, I laid it face down as I went to the closet. Being that it was semi-empty, the bags weren't hard to spot. Plus, they were sitting in the middle of the floor. I looked through the first one and then the second one, seeing that it was Rashad's things in it. When I got to the third one, I heard arguing coming from downstairs and rushed to the door.

Being that Rasheeda had just called her husband on the phone, I knew it wasn't him. It wasn't until I walked out of the bedroom that I recognized the voice to be Rashad's. My heart started racing as my hands trembled. I didn't know what to do. A part of me wanted to hide in the hall bathroom but the other part didn't even want to be in the same house as him. So, I hurriedly ran down the stairs.

He was in the foyer with his mama in his face cursing him out. Being that he was facing toward the stairs, we locked eyes and I stopped in my tracks, unable to move, and it was like his body had frozen as well, as we stared at one another.

"Shit!" I hissed as I snapped back to my senses and tried to dash down the stairs, but it was too late because Rashad was already making his way to me. "Shad, move!" I yelled as he stood in front of me. Sadness and madness filled his eyes, and I didn't know if he was going to beg me to give him a second chance or curse my ass out. Either way, I didn't want to hear any of it.

"Nah... You about to talk to me." He grabbed my arm and tried to pull me up the stairs, but I wouldn't budge.

"Rashad, leave that fucking girl alone! You got some nerve to think she want to talk to you after you married and had kids with her best friend."

"Exactly, so get the hell off me!" I snatched away from him as I agreed with his mama, who was standing at the bottom of the steps.

"Man, I don't wanna hear none of that. Not after you had the nigga to come into my gotdamn house and try to kill me, you owe me a conversation." With that, he leaned down and wrapped his arms around my legs, scooping me up and running up the stairs. It happened so fast that all I could do was scream.

As soon as we made it to the bedroom, he hurriedly closed and locked the door, but his mama was beating on it and twisting the knob before he could even lock it good. She was even yelling for him to open the door before she called the police on his ass. *See?* That was the exact reason I loved Rasheeda. Son or not, she didn't play about me.

"Shad, move!" I motioned like I was about to get off the bed before he pushed me back down and hovered over me.

"Man, cut this bullshit out, Nique. You're pregnant with my fucking child and I need to talk to you about it. For one, I'm not feeling you laying up with that nigga while carrying my seed. You need to bring yo' ass home. I done moved all my clothes and shit out the house, so you can stay there because I'm not about to have you pregnant with my child and staying with that fat ass nigga. You can have the car back and everything."

"Shad, fuck you! I'm not staying in that fucking house! You can take that house and that car and stick 'em up your ass! I don't want shit from you. Not even that gotdamn baby I was pregnant with!"

"What?" He scowled at me. I didn't want to tell him I was no longer pregnant by him, but I thought maybe if I told him I had ended the pregnancy, then maybe he would get the picture that it was over between us, and I had no desire of getting back with him. "Fuck you mean, you didn't want my baby?"

"You heard what the fuck I said. I didn't want it! I don't want shit that has something to do with you."

"So, you telling me that you aborted my child?" He had the nerve to look hurt when he asked that. I didn't verbally answer him, but I gave him a look that said I damn sure did. "Nique, tell me you're playing before I beat yo' ass in here. You did not have a fucking abortion just to be with that black ass nigga."

"No, I had an abortion because I didn't want to be pregnant by you. It had nothing to do with Dyce!" When those words rolled off my tongue, he hauled back with a closed fist like he was about to punch me, but I wasn't about to give him the satisfaction and kneed his ass in the balls as hard as I could.

When he yelled and fell over, grabbing his private part, I made a dash for the door, quickly unlocking it and running out, damn near tackling Rasheeda, who was still standing there, begging him to unlock the door.

I ran down the stairs, damn near falling in the process. After rushing to the living room and grabbing my keys and phone, I ran out the door as Rashad was making his way downstairs, still holding his dick with his mama right behind him, telling him to leave me the hell alone.

I ran out to my truck and hopped in, starting the engine and speeding off as Rashad was running to his car. On the street that his parents lived on, there were so many stop signs that I had to run a few in an attempt to get away from the fool, but he was on my ass.

I didn't want to go to the hotel I was staying at because I didn't want him to know where I was. So, my only resort was to call Dyce. I didn't want to, but I didn't have any other choice. It was clear that Rashad wasn't letting up.

"What's up, Shawty?" Dyce answered the phone.

In a frantic tone, I said, "Dyce, Shad is chasing me and I don't want to go to the hotel because I don't want him to know where I'm staying."

"What?" I repeated myself and he didn't hesitate to tell me to come to him. He said, "I'm at home. Come to my house, now, and stay on the phone with me. Where the fuck you at?" Instantly, his voice had changed from when he first answered. He sounded pissed, and I hated I had to call him and fuck up his mood, but I didn't know what else to do, and I damn sure didn't have anyone else to call.

I guess calling the police would've been the right thing to do, but I felt safer calling Dyce.

"I went by his mama's house because she had been calling me and—"

"Why you didn't tell me that when you called me instead of saying you were on your way back to the hotel? I could've met you there and parked down the street while you went in there and talked to her. You didn't think that nigga was going to come?"

I felt stupid when he asked that, but I really didn't think Rashad would, especially when I told Rasheeda that I didn't want him to know that I was there, and I told Dyce that.

"Man, that mothafucka is going to make me kill his ass for real. Where you at now?" I told him that I was only ten minutes away, and he asked if Rashad was still following me. I said, yes... "Fuck this! Where exactly are you? I'm about to come to you."

"No, bae... I'll be there in a minute. We don't even have to stay on the phone while I—"

"Yes, the fuck we do! Hold on right quick, though." I said, *okay*. I was talking to him on my car radio and took turns looking out the rearview mirror and the side mirror, all the while trying to keep my eyes on the road.

Rashad would get so close up on me at times that I felt he was going to ram into the back of me. He was acting like a fucking lunatic and since all this shit happened between us, Rashad had turned into a man that I didn't even know was in him. No, we hadn't been through anything like this before, but I always thought he was the type that would let go when it was time. Okay, we never planned to break up, but being that he was the cause of our split, it should've been easy for him to just walk away.

"Aye, I'm back. Where you at now?"

"About to turn on your street and he's coming, too. Does he know where you live?"

"Hell nawl! The fuck he needs to know where I live for?" he paused, but not long enough for me to tell him I was just simply asking a question. "When you pull up, don't even get out right away. Just lean back in your seat."

"What? Dyce, what you about to do?"

"Just do what I said, Shawty."

I shook my head. It was too late for me to regret calling him because I was a couple of houses down from his and told him that. All he said was okay and ended the call in my face. When I pulled up and whipped into the driveway, I saw Dyce cocking his gun back... I was so stuck on what I thought was about to go down that I didn't even do as he said and leaned back as I watched him with my mouth open.

It wasn't until he aimed his gun at Rashad's car that had slowed down that I fell over. I didn't hear no gunshots, but I damn sure heard tires screeching away. I took that as Rashad saw the gun and fled for his life.

I remained leaning over my seat until Dyce opened my door and told me that I could get out. I jumped out.

"Go in the house. Let me make sure that nigga doesn't come back." He didn't have to tell me twice. I damn near ran inside, only to get in and stop in my tracks.

"What the hell?" I voiced aloud as my face contorted into a frown. Dyce had me fucked up. Turning around, I motioned like I was about to walk back out the door, only to turn back around and face the woman that was walking from upstairs. She had stopped in her tracks halfway down the stairs and glared at my ass like I had no reason to be in Dyce's house.

"Who are you?" My voice was filled with much anger than I intended for it to be. All I could think about was the message Kelsi had sent me, telling me that Dyce had come from upstairs at his bar with his ex and he was all in her face.

"No, the question is, who are you?" She had the nerve to ask me. I knew Dyce had a sister, and I knew this woman wasn't her. He had shown me pictures of his family. I'd met his brother already, but he still showed me pictures of him, his sister, and his parents. Then, he had already told me that he wasn't close to his other family members—which weren't many.

He came from a small family just like me. The only difference, he had siblings, and I didn't.

"Look, let me get Dyce because I'm not about to play any fucking games!" I turned around to Dyce walking through the front door. I didn't waste no time getting all in his face. I had been played long enough and in the worst way that I wasn't about to let him play me. He had talked all that bullshit about Rashad hurting me, and now he had some other bitch in his house. "Who the fuck is this, Dyce?" I pointed behind me with my thumb.

I was glaring up at him, but his ass wasn't even paying me any attention. He was looking past me, towards the stairs while wearing a hard mug.

"Jay, I know you didn't take your ass upstairs when I told you to stay the fuck down here." He spoke with much venom laced in his voice, almost scaring the shit out of me.

"I had to pee!" The woman, who he'd just called Jay, snapped as she slowly started back walking down the steps. She looked pissed, and I felt I was the only one that had the right to be upset right now. Well, unless he was playing us both. If this was the bitch that Kelsi had told me about, I was done with Dyce's ass.

Still pointing with my thumb as the woman reached the bottom step, I asked Dyce, "Is this the bitch that you had in your office?"

"Bitch? Oh, I got your bitch!" She snapped, then turned to Dyce. "You better get her ass. Clearly, she ain't heard about me and how I get down."

"Aye, man... Shut the fuck up and get out my house." Dyce reached around me and grabbed her by the arm. He looked so upset, and I didn't know if he was still mad about Rashad or about her coming from upstairs.

"No..." She tried snatching away from him, but I guess his grip was too tight because her arm damn sure didn't get out of his grasp. "Dyce, let go of me! We still hadn't talked yet. Whoever she is, she needs to go outside and wait her turn."

"Nah, you about to get the fuck out. Whatever you have to talk to me about, it can wait, but if you're on that bullshit you were on back at the bar about us getting back together, then you might as well save that shit because like I told you, it ain't happening."

"Don't be telling her my damn business." I didn't know if he'd loosen his grip or what, but she was able to get out of his hold, throwing one of her hands on her hips as she shifted all her weight to one side. "And it's not about that. I wanted to tell you that I was moving back here. My grandma is getting older and I'm going to move into her apartment with her until we can find a house."

"Okay, and?"

She looked from him to me, and then back to him. Clearly, she didn't want me to hear their conversation, and I didn't care to hear it, either. I'd already heard enough. She was the one he had up in his office. I knew sooner or later it would come to light. I just didn't think it would be this soon.

While a part of me wanted to walk out and leave, the other part wanted to know what in the hell was going on. Well, it was obvious from what Dyce had said to her, but I wanted to hear more. I wanted to know if he really didn't want her back or if he was just saying that because I was here.

I might've been upset that he had another woman in his house, but my heart really didn't want to believe Dyce was that type. However, after what Rashad had done, I didn't put shit past anyone.

"Can you tell her to give us some privacy?" The woman, Jay, snapped her head around to look at me, giving me the stank face. "Like, I don't know who you supposed to be to him, but me and him have history together."

"Well, me and him are making history now!" I let be known, not even knowing what made me say that or where it had come from. I just prayed it didn't come back and bite me in the ass. "So, whatever you got to say, you might as well say it because I'm not going nowhere!"

She looked at Dyce when I said that like she was expecting him to check me, but he said nothing as his tongue brushed over his lips. There was a moment of silence, and I couldn't even believe how I was acting over this man. I was fresh out of a relationship with a semi still broken heart. I had no room to be going back and forth over another man. Shit, I still had to beat the brakes off Beauti and if this bitch didn't fix her damn attitude and stop coming at me sideways, then I would more than likely have to beat her ass, too, and then leave Dyce along for good for having me fighting over him.

"Look, if you're going to tell me what you're telling me that for, then tell me. If not, then get the fuck out so I can talk to my girl."

"Your girl?" She wasn't the only one shocked. I was too. Yes, me and Dyce had been kicking it heavy and getting to know one another better but to hear him refer to me as his girl did something to me. As butterflies settled in the pit of my stomach, I pushed the corner of my bottom lip into my mouth to keep from blushing, refusing to let her see how that made me feel.

"You heard what the fuck I said! Now, whatever you gotta say, say the shit or bounce."

Her eyes narrowed as she scowled at Dyce. She didn't speak up right away, as if she was contemplating whether she wanted to say whatever it was in front of me or not. She had no other choice because I wasn't going anywhere and had made that clear. Not only did I, but Dyce did, too.

Saying fuck it, she explained without a care in the world, "Well, I was trying to see if we could stay over here until we found a house. That way, we won't have to stay in her apartment, plus..." She cut her eyes at me and then averted them back to him. "It will give us time to talk about us."

"Man..." Dyce sang as I chuckled, wanting to tell her ass there wasn't shit to talk about when it came to them. However, I didn't want to put my foot in my mouth. Yes, he had just referred to me as *his girl*, but I still didn't know for sure where we stood. We hadn't even talked about making things official between us.

"See, that's why I wanted to talk to you in private because I knew you were going to be acting all funny and shit in front of this—"

"In front of this what?" I had just had an abortion the other day and I didn't think I should've been fighting, but if she thought she was about to stand here and call me out my name when she didn't even know me, nor had I done anything to her, she was in for a rude awakening.

"Girl, look—"

"Nah, you look!" Dyce interrupted her. "It's time for you to leave, Jay. I told you back at my office that it ain't nothing to discuss when it comes to us. We ain't getting back together and I love yo' grandma and everything, but ya'll ain't about to come here. The fuck this look like, a fucking hotel?"

"Really, Dyce? You about to do me like that?"

"Man, just get the fuck up out of my house, and don't come back over here." Walking over to the door, he opened it and took a step back so she could leave, letting her know there was nothing else to talk about. She looked over at me, glaring at my ass through narrowed eyes before turning back to look at Dyce, not bothering to leave. She had a look on her face like she wanted to beg him to get back with her or to let her move in with him, but Dyce displayed a mug on his face, letting her know that he didn't want to hear shit else she had to say.

"You know what? Fuck this and fuck you, Dyce! I can't believe you're trying to play me for this bitch." I dropped my keys and motioned toward her, only for Dyce to be a little quicker at getting to me before I could get to her. It was like he was expecting me to beat her ass or something because he was a little too quick for me.

"Aye, chill the fuck out, Shawty!" He whispered in my ear as he swept me off my feet. "Get the fuck out, Jordyn!"

"Fuck you and that bitch!" She said the B-word hard, letting me know she meant that. I called her ass one right back as she was leaving out the house, slamming the door behind her. I was already upset with Rashad, and she had only added to the madness.

Wiggling out Dyce's arms, I turned to face him instead of

running out the door after his ex. She was a non-factor, so I wasn't really worried about her.

"Why was she even over here?" I questioned as I looked up at him, scowling like I was ready to swing on his ass.

"Man, I don't know. She called me and told me that she was here and when I got here and asked what the fuck she was doing at my house, you called, telling me that nigga was chasing you. I didn't even have time to make her ass leave."

"Why was she coming from upstairs?" I folded my arms over my breast as I awaited his answer."

"I don't fucking know, Unique." Dyce had the nerve to sound annoyed with me as he took a seat on the third step.

"Yeah, sure you don't. It's funny that you had her up in your office and now at your house, coming from all upstairs and shit. I been knew about her, but I was trying to give your ass the benefit of the doubt."

"You don't think I knew you heard about her?" He looked at me like I was crazy, causing me to drop my head. "Kelsi was there, so I knew her ass had told you, but I didn't think you were dumb enough to believe I was up there fucking with the damn girl. As much shit as I talked about that nigga and how he did you, you really think I'm about to be on that bullshit?"

I couldn't even say shit when he asked that, because right now, I felt ridiculous. Pushing my bottom lip between my teeth, I bit down on it as I continue staring at the floor. I was so embarrassed I even brought it up that I just wanted to leave.

"So, you ain't got shit to say now, huh? You were just all mouth seconds ago." He asked, antagonizing me. I felt like a child, and he was right; I didn't have anything to say, but I knew he wanted me to react. Maybe to even express how I felt about his ex trying to get back with him. "Whatever you got to say, you better go ahead and say the shit now. I don't want to hear shit else about it later on."

This time, I couldn't hold my tongue. He had me fucked up.

Yes, I felt like a child who was getting chastised, but I wasn't a child.

"Wait a minute, Dyce, I'm not your child. So, you're not about to try to tell me when I can say something and when I can't. The fuck!"

"When it comes to me cheating or doing some fuck shit to you, I am!" He paused, glaring at me like he was expecting me to voice a response, but I didn't. "One thing I'm not about to have is a mothafucka accusing me of doing some shit I didn't do... Not one that I'm fucking with heavy! I don't care what yo' home girl thought she saw or ran back and told you, but I'm not about to have you accusing me of shit that you know damn well I'm not doing."

"But you know what I've been through, Dyce. So, you can't fault me for having trust issues."

He ran his tongue over his lips before speaking. "And I get that. I guess I don't blame you for having your guard up, but at the same time, I don't want to be getting accused, either. I told you about my ex and how she stayed accusing a nigga. I don't tolerate that bullshit because I know I'm not that type of man and I would like to hope you know that, too."

I dropped my head. Did I believe Dyce was that type? Of course not. It was just; I had been through a lot, and I didn't want to end back up in the same predicament. My heart was fragile right now and hell, I would like to hope Dyce understood that. Even so, I knew I didn't want to lose him.

"I'm just scared, Dyce..." I finally responded after what seemed like forever.

"I know you are..." Reaching out for me, he pulled me into his arms, surprising me because I didn't even know I was that close to him for him to grab me, but he did. My arms automatically draped around his neck, but I didn't close in for a kiss. I just stared into his eyes as he did me. "But I want you to know, I ain't here to cause you any pain. I only want the best for you, Shawty, because I know you deserve that. Like I told you, even if we don't end up together, I still want that, and nothing about the way I feel for you would change Because I know you ain't tryna rush into anything."

"I wasn't..." I voiced, shocking myself, but I didn't regret the words. "But I'm not trying to lose you."

"And you won't!"

My lips twisted from side to side as I took in a deep breath, only to release it. I then pushed my bottom lip into my mouth as I closed my eyes, thinking hard about my next few words. As I stated, my heart was fragile, but I couldn't deny there was something I felt for Dyce that couldn't be ignored. The butterflies he gave me were out of this world and I was slowly losing the battle of fighting the way I really felt about him.

Well, honestly, I had lost that fight.

"I'm in love, Dyce..." Slowly, I reopened my eyes to see that his was still locked on me. His face held the same expression, almost scaring me because I couldn't read through his ass. While a part of me wanted to have some type of regret that I'd used the L-word, the other part didn't regret it at all. I needed him to know, even if he wasn't on that level. At least I knew for sure that he felt something for me and even if it wasn't love, in my heart I knew it was close to being. "I wasn't supposed to have fallen for you this soon and though I hate it, my heart had a mind of its own and I can't help what I feel for you. So, again, I'm scared because even though I feel you won't do me wrong and you might be the best thing that could've ever happened to me, it's just..."

I dropped my head and shook it, but Dyce wanted me to let him know what I felt.

He asked, "It's just, what?"

"Too gotdamn soon, and that's what scares me."

"That shit is understandable, but it happens. You think I was tryna fall in love with yo' ass?" I blinked my eyes a few times and just stared at me as his tongue leisurely moved across his lips. I wanted to kiss him so bad, but I knew I would want more after the kiss, and being that I'd just had the abortion a couple of days ago, I couldn't have sex. I was still spotting from it. "Shit happens and I don't regret the way I feel about you."

I pushed a weak smile onto my face as I went in for a kiss. I couldn't help myself after hearing he had no regrets about falling in love with me. Parting my lips with his tongue, he pushed it deep down my throat as he kissed me hard. Dyce's arms went around my waist as he pulled me in between his legs. By now, I was on my knees in front of him, kissing him just as hard as he kissed me. It was so passionate that I was emitting low moans against his mouth that grew louder as he palmed my ass.

Our bodies were so close that I felt his dick grow harder and harder as we tongue one another down. Without my consent, my hand found its way between us, and I had his massive dick in my hand, stroking it through the sweats he wore. He had put them on before he left me this morning.

"Shit..." Dyce groan as I slowly stroked his dick before pulling back from the kiss. I might not have been able to have sex, but that didn't mean I couldn't please him. Pushing back, he rested his forearm on the step above him and watched me as I pulled at the hem of his pants along with his boxer briefs, freeing his dick.

It was so hard and thick that my fingers couldn't even connect while my hand was wrapped around it. Just the sight of it made my mouth water. I licked the head before taking him into my mouth. Immediately, we both let out moans as I pleased him until he reached his peak.

I allowed Dyce to explode in my mouth. I wasn't a swallower and let it just ooze out of my mouth as I licked around the sensitive head of his dick until he could no longer stand it and gently pushed my head back.

"Shiiitttt!" I giggled as Dyce said that. Wiping my mouth, I stood and told him that I was going into the bathroom to clean myself up.

Inside the downstairs bathroom, I washed my mouth with water before dashing water on my face. I was going right back to the hotel, so I knew I would be able to brush my teeth and wash my face when I got back there. When I walked back out, Dyce was still sitting on the stairs, stuck in a trance.

Laughing, I asked, "You good?"

"Mannnn... You know I don't be trying to take naps and shit, but right now, a nigga need one from the spell you just put on my ass."

I giggled. "Well, I'm just paying you back from all the ones you've been putting on me, and, you know I'm always down for an afternoon nap." I wasn't sleepy at all, and I knew all the naps I'd been taking before were only because I was pregnant. However, there was no doubt in my mind that once I laid in his muscular arms, I would be out like a baby.

"Let me lock up my house and hit this blunt right quick. I'll be up there in a minute."

I said okay, and then headed up the steps after picking up my keys. While in his bedroom, I stripped out of my clothes and then went into the bathroom. When I was walking out, Dyce was walking in.

"Dang, that was quick," I told him. "I was hoping to steal a pair of shorts or something."

"Girl, now you know damn well you can't—"

"I know I can't fit them, but I was going to make it work. Being that I had no plans of coming to your place and going to sleep, I didn't bring myself anything to sleep in." I was spotting and didn't want to get into his bed like this. After he told me to help myself and went into the bathroom, I walked over to the drawer he pointed to. I tried to find the smallest pair of his boxer's briefs but had no luck. So, I just grabbed a pair and had to tie it on the side.

As I told him, I made it work, causing him to laugh when he came out of the bathroom after taking a quick shower.

I had just spat his nut back on his dick, so it was understandable that he wanted to clean it off. Hell, I had washed my face and used some of his mouthwash while I was inside.

Once we were in his bed and I was in his arms, facing him, he kissed the tip of my nose, then told me, "I wanna take you out, Nique. Like, on a date to a nice ass restaurant. You've been through so much and stressing like a mothafucka that I just want you to enjoy yourself. I was thinking about tonight, but nah, I wanna do something tomorrow. In the morning, I want us to go somewhere and eat breakfast. I wanna take you to get a massage, get your hair done, and your nails and feet so I can kiss on them because right now they're kind of busted."

"What?" I damn near shouted. "Boy, my feet are not busted. They might need to be done, but they're not busted." I rolled my eyes at him while laughing. I felt a little embarrassed because I was so used to my feet being done. Kelsi used to always keep my shit hooked up, but now that I wasn't cool with her ass anymore, I was going to have to pay someone to do them, and right now, I just didn't have the funds.

"Nah, I was just playing because you know I would still put them in my mouth. But for real, I just wanna treat you out. You cool with that? We can even hit up the mall and do some shopping. I know I need to get me some more shit and I'm pretty sure you can find something to get."

I shifted and didn't speak up right now. I hated that I had so much damn pride. This man wanted to, clearly, give me the world, but I was so hesitant to receive it. I was crazy for that, I know, but I just couldn't help the way I was.

After a while of silence, I told him, "Well, I have a lot of clothes back at my old place. I just haven't been having the time to go get them."

"You hadn't been having the time, or you been scared of that nigga."

"More like I don't want to deal with him." Dyce nodded his head up and down but didn't say anything. "He told me at his mama's house that he had moved out the house and I could move back in. He even said I could have the car back, too, but I told that nigga, he could take that house and car and stick it up his ass. I just want my damn clothes from in there."

"Well, you know if you want your shit, I don't have no problem taking you to get it. Anytime you want to go, just let me know." I didn't bother responding to that because I already knew I wasn't taking him up on his offer. "In the meantime, I can buy you whatever you need. We can go shopping tomorrow."

"Okay..." I finally agreed, pushing a weak smile onto my face. There was a moment of silence as I stared at Dyce. He watched me as long as he could before closing his eyes. I stretched my neck and kissed his lips. With each peck I gave him, I felt him puckering his lips to kiss me back.

I didn't know who slipped their tongue into whose mouth first. All I knew was, we ended up making out. I poured my heart and soul into kissing Dyce, wanting him to know that everything I said downstairs, I meant it.

9
THE LAST STRAW!

Beauti Woods-Russell

Two Weeks Later...
My husband was asleep on the bed with Lovely laying on his chest While I had Bernard in my arms. I looked down at him and just smiled before kissing him on the neck, causing him to squirm in my arms. His little eyes were opened and looking dead at me, looking just like his dad.

At least, to me, he did. Rashad said he couldn't really tell, yet.

Taking in a deep breath as I looked up at my husband and daughter, my smile grew wider as my heart fluttered. I cherished these moments. Since my daughter had come home, my whole life felt complete. I felt Rashad had been a little distant toward me, but I was trying to ignore it. I felt he just had a lot on his mind. I mean, our daughter was sick and on top of that, we both had been walking around here with sickle cell traits and didn't know it.

He even told me that his mama revealed she, too, had it and

knew he did. Rashad was really pissed about that, and I felt he had every right to be. He told me that he was taking me to his parent's house as his wife instead of Unique's best friend, and I couldn't wait because I had a lot to say to his mama for keeping that from him. Well, I invited myself because he said he wanted to take the twins, but there was no way in hell my babies were going, and I wasn't.

That day would've been a cold day in hell.

I was his wife. He was spending the rest of his life with me. Therefore, I had the right to chill with my in-laws. Rashad was lucky that I had even let all this time go by without meeting them. Being the good wife that I was, I was giving him the opportunity of letting that bitch, Unique, find everything out before we took it to his parents because that was what he wanted.

I didn't care one way or the other.

Walking over to the bed, I took a seat on my side and laid my son down beside his dad. I then reached on the nightstand and grabbed my phone and started taking pictures. I must've had a million pictures stored on my phone and iPad of my family.

It was what I'd dreamed about since childhood; to have an amazing husband and kids.

"Baby... Wake up..." After taking pictures, I sat my phone down and positioned myself to lay on my side, reaching over to rub the side of Rashad's face, causing him to stir in his sleep. His eyes batted before he opened them. Stretching as he placed his hand on Lovely's back to make sure she wouldn't fall off his chest, he looked over at me and then directed his eyes to our son, who was laying on his back and fighting the air.

Bernard was growing so much. Lovely was, too. I just hated how sick my baby was, and her asthma was so bad that she had to get a treatment every night for it.

"What's up? Why ya'll up so early?" He asked me before kissing Lovely on the forehead.

"It's not early. It's after ten, and you need to stop sleeping with her on your chest. You've already spoiled her and now when you're not here, I have to walk around with her in my arms until you come home," I fussed. Lovely was so spoiled by Rashad that it didn't make any sense.

"She'll be alright. She knows she can always lay on daddy's chest." He kissed the top of her head.

"Well, mama is going to want to lay on it tonight. So, she's going to have to get in her bassinet." I rolled my eyes, causing Rashad to chuckle. I had one more week before my six weeks check-up, but since I was no longer bleeding, Rashad and me had sex the other night.

I know, I know… I had no business having sex, but I was horny, and I knew he was, too, and I wasn't about to let my man continue walking around with a hard dick. Plus, I had been giving him head so much that I was tired of it. Don't get me wrong, I loved the taste of my husband's dick, but I wanted to feel him inside of me.

Sex with him was everything—which, it always had been. This time, though, he penetrated me nice and slowly from the side as he kissed the back of my neck and cupped my breast. We professed our love for one another, me more than him, but I knew he loved me and felt the same, nonetheless. He was spending more time telling me how good my pussy felt and how much he missed it.

I knew he did… just as much as I missed his dick being inside of me.

"So, what time are we going to your parent's house, I need you to call and see if there's anything I need to bring. I want to get there early so I can see if she needs me to help her with anything," I ranted all in one breath. I was so excited, yet, nervous to go there as his wife. I knew there were going to be so many questions about me and Rashad, and I was prepared to answer them all. I just prayed it wouldn't be awkward being that they loved Unique so much.

They never had a problem with me, but I didn't want them to dislike me because of the situation.

"I'm pretty sure she'll be okay, and she won't need you to bring anything. She cooks every Sunday, so she'll be alright."

"But, Shad, I'm going there as your wife. I want to make a good impression as her daughter in law..." My word trailed off as he brushed his hand over his face and huffed out a deep breath. "What the hell is all that for?"

"Beauti, she doesn't even know you're coming over. I didn't tell her that I couldn't bring the kids unless I brought you."

"What?" I yelled so loud that my daughter started moving like she was about to wake up. I even startled Bernard. Right now, I was upset and didn't even care and continued yelling. "What in the hell you mean you didn't tell her I was coming? You should've told her that when she first asked you to bring my kids over there."

"Stop all that fucking screaming. You scaring my gotdamn kids."

"I don't give a fuck about that!" I made clear as I got off the bed. "All this time you been telling me that she was cooking for us, only to tell me that she doesn't even know I'm coming. You foul as fuck for that! Why the hell would you even do that? You were just going to have me popping up at them folks' house all uninvited and shit."

I watched Rashad as he slowly sat up with Lovely still in his arms. He laid her in her bassinet when he was on his feet and then grabbed his phone off the nightstand and tried to walk out of the bedroom to get away from me, but I wasn't having that. Even with him trying to slam the door in my face, I was hot on his heels.

"So, you ain't going to say shit?"

"Say what, Beauti?" His voice was calm... too damn calm, making me even more upset.

"Something, nigga!" I pushed him as he reached the couch, causing him to fall on it and yell, *what the fuck?* He looked up at me like he wanted to hit me, but I dared him to. I had 911 on speed dial for his ass. "You need to call your mama right now and tell her that I'm coming over there with you and the twins or they ain't coming."

I stood over him as he sat up on the couch and started going through his phone. I wanted to snatch it from his hand, but I didn't because I was expecting him to call her, but he didn't, and he made it clear that he wasn't.

Looking up at me, he said, "Man, you always trying to make something out of nothing and I'm fucking sick of it. I told you I was taking you with us, but now, I ain't taking you no fucking where. The reason I didn't tell my mama is because she doesn't want your ass over there. You were my girl's best friend, and we got married. So, hell no, my mama doesn't like yo' ass for that, and she probably never will. The only reason she's even willing to accept the kids is because they're mine and she wants to get to know her grandkids."

"The only reason she is willing to accept my kids?" I echoed those words as if they were a bad taste in my mouth. "Let me tell you and your mammy something... She doesn't ever have to accept my gotdamn kids. I don't give a fuck if they are yours. If she's not willing to accept me, then she won't be a part of my kid's life, and you should've checked her ass. I'm your damn wife, regardless of who I used to be best friends with."

"What?" The mug on Rashad's face hardened as he looked at me like he couldn't believe I had just said that.

"You heard what the fuck I said!" With a roll of my eyes, I turned around and walked off, heading back toward the bedroom. I heard Rashad say what sounded like, *I better get the fuck out of his face.* I continued walking as I threw up my middle finger and told him. "Fuck you... you and that bitch!" I was talking about his mama, and I was pretty sure he knew it.

Going into my bedroom, I slammed my door shut and locked it. While my son was quiet, Lovely was crying in her bassinet—which was why I even came back to the room in the first place. Had her little spoiled ass not been crying, I damn sure would've stayed in her daddy's face until I got my point across. His ass needed to man up when it came to me, *his wife*. It was bad enough that he had been disrespectful when it came to me since Unique had come home, but I'm not going for him letting his family disrespect me. Mama or not, he needed to check her ass.

I was his wife and came before everybody.

"Lovely, come on, girl." I fussed at my daughter as I rocked her in my arms, trying to give her, her pacifier. She would suck on it for a while only to spit it out and start back crying and I knew it was because she wanted her dad to hold her. If I wasn't so upset with Rashad, I damn sure would've taken her out there to him.

Instead, I walked out of the room to make her a bottle, not even bothering to look Rashad's way. A part of me thought he would say something about Lovely crying, but he didn't. Any other time, he would come get her out of my arms, but this time, he acted like he didn't even hear her.

Back in the room, I fed Lovely and laid down with her until she was asleep. Bernard had fallen asleep on his own while I was in the living room with Rashad, arguing. After laying her down, I went into the bathroom to shower. When I was done, I started getting my kids dressed. I was sure to make a lot of noise as I walked back and forth from my bedroom to theirs.

Not once did Rashad say anything to me.

"Ya'll ready to go see ya'll real grandma?" I asked my kids once I had them in the living room and their car seats. I said it because I knew for sure it would get a reaction out of Rashad since he wanted to sit his mad ass on the couch like he didn't know I was leaving.

"The fuck is that supposed to mean?" I succeeded in getting a reaction from his ass, and just as he had been giving me the silent treatment, I did him the same. "Say, Beauti. What the fuck is that supposed to mean? Talking about, their real grandma. Like my mama ain't shit to them."

Grabbing both of the car seats after throwing the two bags over my shoulder, one that I had packed for them and the other one with Lovely's breathing machine, I opened the door. As I was walking out of the house, I told Rashad, "Boy, fuck you and your bitch ass, bald-headed ass mama!"

Mrs. Sally and her granddaughter were walking out of her house when I said that. I didn't care one bit that they heard me tell my husband that. Right now, it was fuck him and his mama and I meant that.

Slamming the door behind me, I said a small prayer that I wouldn't fall down the stairs as I carried my kids. I had never left the house with them by myself, and I was a little scared too. For the past two weeks, I had been chilling in the house with my husband, trying to rekindle our love. My mama had been calling to see the kids, and I told her last night that when I left my in-law's house, I would come there. I planned to go with Rashad so my family could get to know him as my man and accept my marriage, but clearly, that wasn't going to happen.

"Jordyn, help her with the babies," Mrs. Sally ordered her granddaughter. I didn't say anything, though I wanted to tell her no. Walking over to me, she reached out for the car seat, and I gave her Bernard.

As soon as we hit the bottom step, I reached for the car seat and walked off without even telling her thanks. I didn't know what it was about her, but I just wasn't feeling her.

"You're welcome!" I heard her say, but I ignored her ass. She could kiss my ass, too.

After strapping my kids down, I got in my car and drove off while Mrs. Sally and her granddaughter were still sitting there. I didn't know what was taking them so long to leave, but I didn't care.

Arriving at my parents' house, I frowned when I saw she had company. It was a Range Rover parked in front of the house and though I didn't know who it was; I frowned. I wasn't in the mood for any of her company, especially any of her nosey-ass friends worrying about me and my kids.

Even so, I got on out of the car and didn't bother calling my mama to tell her that I was outside. She didn't have nearly as many steps as me, so I carried both, Bernard and Lovely, up the stairs and had plans of going back to the car to get their bags.

Sitting the twins' car seat on the porch, something told me to twist the knob before knocking. Surprisingly, it was unlocked. I assumed it was because she had company and she just didn't lock it back.

"Ma..." I called out as I walked in, closing the door with my foot. Just as I rounded the corner to the living room, my mama was standing and staring my way through widened eyes. She looked stunned to see me and her behavior caused me to look at the person sitting on the couch beside her.

Unique was looking dead at me. Instantly, my chest started heaving up and down at a rapid pace. Not that I was scared or no shit like that, it was more so that I wanted to beat her ass from the way she tried me when I was giving birth.

I was no longer pregnant, so I dared her to try that shit with me now. However, we were in my parents' house, and I knew she had enough respect to not try no slick shit with me. Plus, she was still sitting down, staring at me. Her not standing made me comfortable enough to sit my babies down and tell my mama,

"I'm going to get their bags. Can you watch them for me tonight?"

Me and Rashad had to have a long talk tonight, and I didn't need no damn kids interfering, crying, and shit.

"Yeah. Go ahead and get the bags. I'll meet you at the door to get them," my mama said in a rushed tone. She was rushing me to leave, and it pissed me off. I felt if anyone needed to leave, it was Unique. I didn't even understand why she was here.

Unique had always thought my parents were hers and I secretly hated her. Hated how sometimes it felt like they had her back more than they did mine. This situation was one of these times. My mama knew all about Unique attacking me at the hospital because I told her last week when she asked if I tried reaching out to her to make amends. All she had to say to that was, I deserved it.

It hurt my feelings because no matter what I had done, she shouldn't have let that leave her mouth. Another thing I didn't like was her always talking about karma and how me and my husband deserved what was going to happen to us. My mama was being real nasty toward me and the only reason I hadn't cut her off was because I needed her when it came to my kids.

Until Rashad got over this little phase he was going through, and we got back to the place we were before his ex got out, I had to kiss my mama's ass and act as if her negativity didn't faze me. Once I had my husband back on board, I was cutting her off, just as I had done with my sister. Hopefully, by then, my in-laws could accept me. If they didn't, fuck them, too!

As I walked off the porch, I heard the front door open and my mama yelling. I turned around just as Unique was making her way down the stairs toward me. I didn't have time to even process what was going on before she grabbed me by my hair.

"Bitch!" That was all she said as her fist pounded against my face. I was trying to swing back, but it was to no avail. "I told you I was gon' beat yo' ass!" I heard her say before I was slung to the ground.

"Let me get up, bitch!" I yelled as I tried reaching out to grab her. I wanted to grab her shirt to pull her down with me, but I also wanted to grab her hands so she could no longer punch me.

She was now getting the best of me right now, and I just wanted a fair fight.

"Hoe... Bitch! You thought I was playing with you?" She fussed, calling me all types of hoes and bitches with each punch. I couldn't believe her ass was still trying to fight over my man. But I guess her ass was in her feelings because the best woman won.

"Nique, come on... That's enough!" After what seemed like forever, I finally heard my mama yell that. It made me wonder where in the hell she had been this whole time because it felt like this fight had been going on forever and not once had she said a word.

"Unique, come on, baby. It's not worth it!" This time, I heard the familiar male tell her. It was my dad, which confused me, being that I didn't even see his car in the driveway. So, I didn't even know he was home.

When I realized I wasn't able to stop Unique from beating my ass, I had no other choice but to try to at least protect my face. When I tried to get in a fetal position, she grabbed me by my hair and drug me from one spot to the other, ignoring me kicking and screaming for her to let me go. Well, she did let me go but only to start back punching my face, leaving me no choice but to lay on my back with my hands up to my face.

I hated she had beat my ass like this. When I was finally able to remove my hand from my face shortly after the punches stopped, I jumped up and looked around the yard for her. My face was stinging, and I had a headache out of this world from her pulling my hair. I had just gone to get my hair plaited four days ago, so I had plaits now laying on the ground and everything.

That pissed me off more because I knew my real hair was attached to them.

"Bitch, you got me fucked up!" I ran toward the end of the driveway where my dad had grabbed Unique and taken her. He was holding her so she wouldn't get away. He had his arms around her like he was consoling her and the icing on the cake was my mama standing there, too, rubbing her back. Nobody was even comforting me, and I was the one that had gotten my ass beat. "The fuck ya'll standing around hugging this bitch for when she just attacked me?"

I kept my distance from them as I talked my shit. Though I wanted to run up on Unique, I was scared she would beat my ass again. No, I had never been scared to fight anyone, but the few fights I had gotten into, I had never lost one. If getting beat up felt like this, I never wanted to get my ass beat again.

The crazy thing about it, Unique, wasn't even a fighter. At least I never saw her fight anyone before, but just so happened, she beat my ass.

If she thought she was going to get away with this shit, she definitely had another thought coming.

"Beauti, just get in your car and leave!" My dad had the nerve to finally walk over to me, pointing at my car as he scowled at me like I was the one that started this fight.

"Get in my car and leave?" I echoed. "So you're making me leave and not her? She was the one that started this shit. She attacked me, but I'm the one that has to leave."

"Bitch, I didn't start shit! I been told your ass that I was fucking you up. I even told your husband and sister the same thing."

"See?" I looked at my dad and then my mama, who had moved in front of Unique. I guess trying to block her from getting to me, even though I was a few feet away from her. "She's standing there disrespecting me, and ya'll okay with this? Bitch can't get mad because my husband doesn't want her ass. What, you mad because

I got the ring, and you didn't?" I looked over at Unique when I stated the last part, provoking her.

It was like I had awakened the beast in her because, though my parents were between us, she was still able to get to me. This time, though, I wasn't caught off guard. I saw her coming and was ready for her.

I didn't know who hit first, but we were in a full brawl until she managed to slang me on the ground again. However, the beating didn't last long before it ended, and I jumped up to see my dad carrying her over to the Range Rover.

Oh, that's her truck. I thought as I picked up a rock and threw it at the truck.

"Fuck you, hoe!" I felt a little bad when I threw the rock at the back window, and it cracked because I wasn't even sure if it was her truck or not. As I stated, my dad's car wasn't in the driveway, and I would hate for it to have been his and I fucked up the window.

But why would he park on the side of the road? Even with me wondering that, I didn't want to cause any more damage to the truck without knowing for sure who it was. So, I just continued fussing and cursing Unique out as my mama grabbed my arm and started pulling me toward the house. I was so upset that I didn't even bother snatching out of her reach.

Inside the house, I started yelling at my mama. "You leaving my kids in here to go out there and comfort that bitch after she attacked me? You and my dad know ya'll wrong. Ya'll stood there and let her jump on me like that." I was yelling so loud that I woke my kids up, but I didn't care.

"Beauti, now wait a minute. I didn't let nobody attack you and I didn't leave your kids in here to go comfort nobody, either. I left them in here to go out there and stop ya'll from acting like kids. Ya'll out there fighting over that no good ass man that doesn't care about either of ya'll."

"You wish he didn't care about me. It makes all ya'll so mad that I have someone that loves me and married me regardless of who he was with and whose feelings got hurt. That shit kills ya'll, doesn't it?"

Before my mama could retort anything, the front door opened and slammed shut. I jumped and looked toward the entrance of the living room, trying to make sure it wasn't Unique coming back for round three. Had it been her, I would've run right into the kitchen, got a knife, and stabbed her ass.

It would've been self-defense, so there was no way in hell I would get any jail time for it.

It was my dad walking in and we made eye contact. I could see in his eyes that he wasn't pleased about what had just gone down, and I could see on his face that I couldn't come at him the same way I just did my mama. Since everything had come out, me and my dad's relationship had been pretty much nonexistent, and my mama only dealt with me because of the twins.

In their eyes, I had betrayed them as well. I disgusted and embarrassed them, but I didn't care. It was my life and how I chose to live had nothing to do with them. I said it once, and I was going to say it again; they were acting like I had gone out and killed someone. The shit I did happened every day. So, they needed to get over it.

With a shake of his head, my dad didn't say anything as he turned around and walked out of the living room. It was at the same time the front door opened again and closed. It was my sister this time.

I guess she felt the tension when she walked in because she looked from me to my mama and asked what was going on. Her eyes lingered on me a while longer. Even when my mama told her that me and Unique had been fighting, she still didn't take her eyes off me.

"Why you looking at me like that, like I started this shit?" I yelled, referring to the fight that had just happened. I was so upset that anyone could get it.

Kelsi responded with, "I didn't even say shit to you, Beauti, but what you mean, like you started this. You did start it."

"Kels, don't even start with me because you did the same shit I did. The only difference is, I ended up marrying Shad." She knew exactly what I was talking about, and my mama did too. I could see her eyes widen from the corner of my eye. "You sitting up here jealous as hell because he wanted to marry me and I don't understand why. You weren't even upset when Nique was with him for ten years, but you want to tell me how wrong I am for marrying him. How about this? You and everybody else that feels a certain way about my marriage can go to hell." With that, I turned on my heels and walked off.

I was done with all their asses and didn't want to hear shit else anybody in that house had to say. All they were doing were pointing fingers at me and it wasn't right.

Inside my car, I grabbed my phone and went to my contact. When I found the number that I was looking for, I hit send but the person didn't answer. So, I went to my message thread.

> Me: You need to call me back ASAP. Today was the last straw. That bitch Nique got to go. Handle it or else...

10

MORE TO EVERY STORY!

Kelsi Woods

I was speechless. I couldn't believe my sister had just outed me like that. After all that I had done for her, keeping her secrets and she put me on the spot. I didn't even know why I was surprised, especially when I felt she had been wanting to tell my darkest secret for the longest.

As my chest heaved up and down at a rapid pace, I stared at the spot Beauti had just walked off from, as if she was still standing there. A huge part of me was glad she was gone because had she still been standing here, I damn sure would've grabbed her ass, and trust me, she didn't want any problems with me.

One thing I knew for certain, Beauti knew how I got down.

"Kelsi, please tell me that you didn't—"

"It was before Nique, ma." I turned to face my mama, interrupting her before she could even finish her sentence. She was already thinking the worst and I guess she had every right to. The way Beauti had just blurted that I'd pretty much slept with

Rashad, too, made it seem like it was while he was with Unique, and that damn sure wasn't the case.

I didn't even want Rashad's ass. It was something that had just happened, and that was it. Where Beauti got the bullshit from that I was jealous he had married her, I didn't know, but she could get it out of her head.

"If it was before her, why is Beauti bringing it up now, as if it happened during the time him and Nique were together?"

"Because she's Beauti, and she wants everybody to look bad with her." My mama's biggest concern was if Unique knew about it or not, and when she asked, all I could do was drop my head and say, "No."

"Kels... Even if it was before her, why wouldn't you tell her?"

"Because?" I took a seat on the couch and pulled over my niece's and nephew's car seats. They were crying and had been since I walked into the house. Being that everybody's mind was messed up and focused on the mess my sister and Rashad had caused, they had ignored the twins, but I was certainly about to get them now.

When my mama saw me getting Lovely out, it hit her that they were crying and she grabbed Bernard.

When we had them somewhat calmed and were able to fix them a bottle, we revisited the conversation. My mama asked, "So, how did you let all these years go by and not tell her?"

"I just didn't think it would ever come up. I mean, me and Shad, both, knew what it was. Neither of us wanted each other, but it came back up when him and Beauti wanted to get married. For some reason, he thought it was okay to tell her and she blackmailed me. She threatened to tell Nique if I didn't agree to be a witness at their wedding, and I just said okay."

"No, you should've went on and let her tell Nique. I would've rather she found out that instead of Beauti marrying that man. You and me, both, know Nique wouldn't have been that mad about you and Shad, being that you said it was before her time. She's understanding and you know that."

"I know..." I dropped my head, looking down at my beautiful niece. She had cried so long that it made me wonder if she needed a treatment. I didn't like the way she was breathing and with her severe asthma, her good-for-nothing ass mama should've made sure she was okay before leaving. "I think Lovely needs a treatment. You want me to get Bernard while you give her one?"

"Yeah, I was just thinking that. Here." We switched the kids and my mama started tending to my niece. As she gave her a treatment, she told me she thought it would be best if I talked to Unique about what was going on, and I agreed. There was a moment of silence between us before she went, "So, that's why you been keeping all this bullshit in, because Beauti is threatened to tell Nique?"

"Yeah, and because she's my sister, too." I jumped my shoulders, lifting my head back up to look at my mama. "I knew things were going to get ugly and Unique would more than likely beat both their asses. I didn't want to cause that. I know I should've told her, but Beauti is my blood sister, and I just didn't want to rat her out and cause a whole bunch of mess. I was put in a tough position, ma. I begged and begged Beauti not to have that man's baby, but she was so set on doing it."

"And you know your sister. When her mind is made up to do something, she is going to do it." She released a heavy breath as she looked down at Lovely and kissed her forehead before bringing her head back up and letting her eyes meet mine. "I don't regret my grand babies being brought into this world, but I just hate it took her being with her best friend's man to create them. This was wrong of Beauti, and I hate how she is going about it."

"Yes!" I agreed with my mama. "She's really blaming us for all this like we were the ones that told her to mess with that man."

"Well, I don't know how much more I can put up with her.

Every time I call her to check on the kids or she calls me, she wants to talk about that no-good-ass man and when I tell her my opinion, which is, they're going to get their karma, she blows up at me. Your dad told me that I need to cut her off until she can get her attitude in check and realize we're not the ones she should be mad with."

"And I agree with him," I let her know. Today was the first time I had talked to Beauti since she showed up at my house and I damn sure wasn't calling her. I was sick of her hanging the shit between me and Rashad over my head. To me, it wasn't even that serious, but I knew it was a must I told Unique before Beauti had the opportunity of doing so.

I knew that would've been right up her alley.

After spending time with my parents and the twins, I decided to leave after a few hours. I had texted Ta before I left and asked him to meet me at my house, but he asked me to come to his instead. So, I headed there once I was inside my car. When I pulled up, he was outside with a couple of his homeboys. I spoke to them and went on inside the house.

Ta had already told me the door was unlocked. I looked around when I got inside as if it was my first time here. He lived in a three-bedroom house, just like me, but his shit was a lot nicer than mine was. Ta had asked me to move in with him a while back, but I declined his offer.

I had never lived with a man before, and taking that step scared me.

I wasn't ready for all that, yet. I had always been the type to have my own shit and giving up my house to move in with someone was something I just wasn't willing to do. However, Ta did help me pay my rent because he was just sweet like that. In all honesty, I kind of felt if we did take things to the next level, it probably would work, but right now, I had a lot on my plate, and it wouldn't have been fair to him if I picked now out of all the times in the world for us to make things official.

There was too much drama in my life. Thanks to my sister.

I was sitting on the couch with my feet tucked underneath me when Ta finally walked in. He was smiling from ear to ear and his eyes were so low that I knew he had been smoking. He was so sexy to me, and I loved how low his eyes got when he was high.

"What's up, baby?" Leaning down before he took a seat, he kissed my lips. As he sat right under me, his head went to the crook of my neck and his hand went in between my thighs. I hadn't even come here for sex.

"Ta, move. I didn't even come here for all that." I giggled, at the same time, moving my neck to the side to give him better access to my neck. My eyes closed as I enjoyed him kissing and sucking on it. I think he did shit like that on purpose. "Move and stop trying to give me a passion mark. I keep telling you, I'm too old to be walking around with that crap."

"Man, ain't nobody trying to give you shit!" Ta lied as he slid off the couch and got down on his knees in front of me, snatching me to the edge of the couch. I automatically unfolded my legs and spread them so that he could make himself comfortable in between them. "I thought you didn't come here for that."

"I didn't." I rolled my eyes as we shared a few pecks. As he unfastened my pants, I kissed all over his face, sucked on his lips and all. I was so turned on by this man that I couldn't wait for him to fuck me. When I felt him tugging at the hem of my pants, I lifted so that he could pull them off, along with my panties.

When they were off, he removed his shirt and unfasten his pants, pulling them down enough to free his dick.

"Ahhhhh." My arms squeezed around his neck as he pushed himself inside of me. His head fell to the crook of my neck as my back arched and my eyes closed. Ta didn't move right away, and neither did I.

"Shiiitttt." Finally, he started stroking his dick in and out of me at a slow pace. I moved my hips with ease, matching his rhythm, as I wrapped my legs around his midsection and locked my feet at the ankle. I was holding him so tight, almost as if I was afraid to let go. "Damn... I can never get enough of this good shit. I'ma make this pussy mine."

"It's already yours!" I felt his head shake when I said that, but I was speaking the truth. My pussy was his. Me and Ta might not have been official, but he was the only man I was sleeping with, and at one time, I knew for a fact that I was the only bitch he was sleeping with.

I never left room for him to fuck anyone else, but I had to admit, lately, I had been off my shit. Dealing with my sister and her shit, I hadn't seen him as much as I wanted, or if I did see him, we wouldn't have sex. I had been taking on more clients just to stay busy. The day Beauti had come to my house, Ta caught bits and pieces of our conversation and he started questioning me on shit I didn't want to reveal to him.

So, I started cutting our time short. Not answering when he called or when he came to the house, I would be sure to have clients there because I'd started working later than I usually would. A couple of times he had come in the middle of the night, but I wouldn't even answer the door for him, and I would even go as far as putting my phone on silent so he wouldn't hear when it rang.

He had gotten tired of my shit and I knew I had to come over here today and let him know why I had been so distant. I refused to let another day go by that I didn't tell him what was really going on.

"If this was my pussy, you wouldn't have been keeping it away for so long." He bit down on my neck hard when he expressed that, causing me to let out a loud, pleasurable whimper. The pain caused my pussy to become wetter as I threw it back to him hard.

He was fucking me hard at this point like he was trying to punish me and my pussy. "You been giving my shit to somebody else?"

"No! Hell no, baby. You're the only one that's getting this."

"Why the fuck you lying to me, Kels? I don't like that shit." I told him that I wasn't, and he smacked my butt and started pulling me toward him with each thrust, telling me that I better not had been lying to him. I wasn't lying, and Ta knew that. He just wanted to talk shit.

I didn't bother asking him if he had been fucking someone else, because honestly, I didn't want to know the answer. Ta was an attractive man, and I knew for a fact, women threw themselves at him all the time, especially that one bitch at Dyce's bar, Nae-Nae. I learned Dyce had fired her for whatever reason, but still... I just knew her and Ta had fucked before.

It was obvious by the way she looked at me and acted toward me anytime she saw me there. Because of that, I loved rubbing it in her face that I was now getting the dick. Even if it wasn't going to be mine forever, I had her in her feelings about it.

Ta kept telling me that he didn't sleep with her, but I knew the real.

"Shit... I'm about to fucking nut, baby... Gotdamn!" As his pace sped up, mine did too. I was reaching my peak and just like any other time, we both released together.

As we sat breathing hard, we shared a passionate kiss before parting.

"That shit is still good," Ta complimented as he pressed down on my knees to stand to his feet. "Shit..." I wanted to laugh at him, almost falling back down, but I didn't. I was too busy trying to figure out why my pussy wouldn't be still good.

I told him, "You're saying that like my shit ain't supposed to be still good."

"Man, don't go getting in yo' feelings. You know I ain't mean nothing by that shit. You need to go clean yourself up?"

"Duh!" I looked up at him like he was crazy. I got up and headed upstairs to his bathroom. Anytime I was here, I never used the downstairs bathroom. It wasn't anything wrong with it, I just rather use the one in his bedroom. After cleaning myself, I walked out of the bathroom to Ta standing at his dresser, still naked and texting on his phone. "Yeah, tell that bitch I'm here right now."

"What?" He jumped and looked back at me. "Fuck is you talking about? I texted that nigga, Dyce."

All I did was press my lips together and gave him a, *yeah right*, look. A bitch wasn't dumb. I had been ignoring him for weeks, so I knew someone else was getting the dick. When he went into the bathroom, leaving his phone on the dresser, I went back downstairs, not even bothering to go through his shit, and I knew he left it there, thinking I would.

Maybe it was Dyce, and he's really not fucking with nobody else. I thought to myself. Even so, I just couldn't make myself think he had gone this long without sex.

Snatching up my pants, I pushed it to the back of my mind. I had to constantly tell myself that Ta wasn't my man, and he could do as he pleased. No, I didn't want him being with another woman and I would certainly be in my feelings and show my ass if I knew for sure that he was.

However, I had no right to.

And no, it wasn't because I wasn't sleeping with nobody else. That was my choice not to, though I knew for a fact that he would be in his feelings, too, if I were sleeping with another man. Our situation was crazy, but it worked for us.

"Why didn't you go through my phone? I left it in there for you to go through it," Ta asked while walking into the living room where I was, now fully dressed. I had my phone in my hand, texting Unique, asking if we could meet up to talk. I prayed she would respond.

"Boy, when have I ever went through your shit? I'm not even

that type, and you know it." I sucked my teeth as my eyes rolled. It was at the same time he was walking over to the couch. Laughing as he flopped down, he slapped my thigh and told me he was just playing.

"So, what's up? What brought you by after all this time of not fucking with me?"

"Don't do that..." I shot back. I knew Ta, and I knew he wanted to make me feel bad for not seeing him as much as I had been. "I told you I've taken on a few more clients, so I've been busy. Plus, dealing with a lot of other shit, too. That's why I came to talk to you today. I'm ready to just lay it all on the table."

After taking in a deep breath, I told Ta everything, and by the time I was done, he was speechless. All he could do was shake his head.

"So, what you think about all this?" I asked, unsure if I even wanted to know how he felt. I took full responsibility for what I did, and all I wanted was a chance to tell Unique my side of the story.

Washing his hand down his face, Ta told me that he thought it would be best that I talked to Unique. He also expressed how he didn't understand why it was so hard for me to tell Unique I had slept with Rashad if it was before her. He had the nerve to insinuate I was lying about when it was and how many times it happened, but I swore to him that I had only slept with that man once.

"You make yourself look guilty as fuck. If that was your homegirl, you should've told her when she first came to you and told you about the nigga. You gave him and your sister some shit to hold over your head when you didn't have to."

"I know..." I mumbled as I dropped my head and released a heavy sigh. When I brought my head back to look at him, I asked, "Do you think Nique would forgive me for my part in all this?"

"Man, I don't even know, Shawty. I mean, you have to look at it from Shawty's perspective. You kept some shit from her, just so she wouldn't know you fucked her nigga before he was even hers. The shit was dumb and the bullshit ass reason you chose not to tell her might have her not wanting to fuck with you again."

"But I—"

"Nah, Shawty." He interrupted me, shaking his head. "I ain't the one that you need to be explaining this shit too. You might as well call her and tell her. I'm over ya'll bullshit. The shit is getting messier and messier and on some real shit, none of ya'll mothafuckas can be trusted."

"I can be trusted!" I rolled my eyes. "But she won't answer the phone for me. Can you call Dyce, please? Just see if she's with him and if he'll let—"

"Man, I ain't doing no kiddie ass shit like that, and I damn sure ain't putting that man in the middle of this shit. If I don't want to be in the middle of it, then what makes you think he would?"

I sucked my teeth at his ass in response. Ta was being childish right now. I wasn't even trying to put them in the middle of it and I honestly didn't get how he felt I was, by only asking him to call Dyce and see if he'll let me talk to Unique. But it is what it is.

One thing I wasn't about to do, was beg him to do shit for me.

"Whatever. I guess I'm about to go home. I'll just call you later or something." He said okay and it kind of hurt my feelings that he didn't ask me to stay. At the same time, I knew it was the middle of the day and he more than likely, wasn't in for the day.

After leaving Ta's house, I stopped and got myself something to eat and then headed home. I just wanted to relax in my bed and watch movies all day since I had no clients. However, when I pulled up to my house, I saw that I had company, and it surprised me because I purposely didn't book anyone today.

It wasn't until I pulled into my driveway and got out that the driver's door opened to the Range Rover, and I saw it was Unique.

Instantly, my heart started racing as I stood at the back of my car, watching as she got out.

I didn't know what to make of her being here, but I silently thanked God that she was here, especially after her and my sister's fight. Deep inside, I prayed she wasn't here to try to fight me because I damn sure didn't think it was one, she would win. I wasn't even trying to fight Unique, though. She was the victim here, and I had to remember that.

11

CELEBRATION GONE BAD!

Unique James

I didn't know why I was here or what even lead me to come to this bitch's house. I guess a part of me wanted to hear her '*side of the* story', as she called it. She had been messaging me on Facebook, begging for me to let her explain herself to me since all this bullshit went down, but I didn't want to hear shit she had to say.

Why I decided to come today was beyond me. After I finally got my hands on her snake-ass sister, I went back to my hotel and showered. I was laying down on the bed, debating if I wanted to call Dyce and tell him about the fight and the bitch cracking my back window with a rock. I didn't feel bad for the fight because I had already made it clear to him and whoever else would listen that I was dragging the fuck out of Beauti, but it was the damage she had done to my truck that had me not wanting to tell him.

However, I knew I had to.

We made a promise to one another to not keep any secrets. Plus, I knew he would eventually find out about it.

"Hey, Nique..." Kelsi spoke in a shaky voice once I got out of my truck. I didn't bother speaking back as I approached her, making sure to keep my distance. I was afraid had I gotten too close, I would end up punching her ass for playing in my face the way she had been doing. "I'm glad you decided to come over."

"I only came to hear this side of the story you claim you wanted to tell."

"Okay, we can go in and talk." She started walking toward the house, but when I said no, she stopped in her tracks. "Okay. Cool. We can talk out here."

There was a moment of silence as she dropped her head. My eyes watered, but I refused to let her see me cry. "How could you know something like that and didn't tell me, Kels? I don't care if Beauti is your sister, you knew this shit was wrong and—"

"Nique, before you met Shad, I slept with him." She cut me off.

"What?"

"Yeah. It was only a one-time thing, and it never happened again. We met at a party, and I went home with him on some drunk shit. A year later, you introduced him to us as your man."

"And you didn't think to pull me to the side and tell me that you had fucked him?"

"I did, but I saw how you were with him. You seemed so happy, and I already knew you were in love because you told me and Beauti that before we even met him." I paused, swallowing hard as I shook my head. "To be honest, I never even talked to him after that night. I mean, when we saw one another, we would speak and keep it moving. That night meant nothing, and that's why I didn't think it was important to tell you, but he mentioned it to my sister for whatever reason, and she threatened to tell you if I didn't be a witness at their wedding. I know I should've told you, but you were just so happy with him, and I didn't want to ruin that for you."

Kelsi was crying, and as bad as I didn't want to feel bad for her, I did. I could see the sincerity in her eyes and knew she was meaning every word. I could see how much this hurt her, but at the same time, she had brought it on herself.

"This shit is unreal." I shook my head as I laughed to myself. Everything was getting crazier, and I was just here... stuck in the middle.

"Nique, I swear, if I would've known all this shit was going to happen, I would've told you about me and Shad. I just..." She paused, dropping her head, only to lift it right back up. "It meant nothing to me. I never thought he would tell my sister and I damn sure would've never thought she would use it against me to get what she wanted. If it means anything to you, there wasn't a day that went by I didn't tell Beauti how wrong she was. I even begged her not to have his kids, but she just didn't want to listen. You know how Beauti is; whatever she wants, she has to have it. Unfortunately, it was Shad this time."

I rubbed my temple as my eyes squeezed shut. This shit just wasn't making sense to me. If Beauti wanted Rashad, all she had to do was tell me and I would've let her have his ass. No, we wouldn't have remained friends, but I would've respected her more if she would've come to me like a woman and told me what was going on.

It damn sure would've saved me a lot of embarrassment.

"I can't do this shit, Kels... Like, man... You know you could've come to me about this. You slept with the man before me, so what in the hell could I have possibly done about that? Shit, he could've come to me, but seeing how he's been moving, I see why he didn't. The nigga is probably walking around with his dick in his hand because he had all three of us. Then your dumb ass sister decided to marry his ass."

"Exactly, knowing I was with him one night and you've spent ten years with him." Kelsi co-signed, shaking her head.

"Now she wants to tell me that I'm jealous because he married her."

Chuckling, I let her know that Beauti had told me the same thing When I beat her ass. I glared at her, waiting to see if she would react to me fighting her sister, but she didn't. I even added, "I'm not done with her ass, either. Every time I see, her, it's on."

"Well, I don't have anything to do with that." Kelsi shrugged. "I don't know what type of spell Shad has on her, but she is cutting everybody off for him when she shouldn't. I don't know if you know or not, but my niece has been diagnosed with sickle cell. My mama told me that she got it from Shad and my sister. They have—"

"Shad doesn't have sickle cell..." At least I had never heard about him having it, and I had been with him for ten years.

"He does. Being that my niece has the disease, he got tested and found out that he carries the trait. My sister found out when she was still in the hospital after giving birth."

"Damn, really?" I felt sorry for the baby, but in no way, shape or form did I feel sorry for them. I wasn't trying to sound harsh, but I felt all this was their karma for doing me dirty.

"And, if you're really pregnant and it's his baby—"

"What you mean; if I'm really pregnant and it's his baby? Who the hell else am I supposed to be pregnant by, Kels?" I tilted my head to the side as I awaited her answer. I knew she was thinking it was by Dyce being that she knew I was fucking around with him. When she opened her mouth to speak, the dumbfounded expression coating her face let me know she was about to play stupid. So, I just held up my hand to hush her. "You know what, don't even answer that because it doesn't even matter, anyway. I guess, thanks for letting me know your side of the story or whatever, but even with me knowing it, I still can't fuck with you. My feelings might change in the future, but right now, I can't rock with none of ya'll."

"Okay... I can respect that." There was so much hurt heard in her voice, but I wasn't about to acknowledge it. Nobody cared about my feelings when they were playing in my face. Taking in all the air I could muster up, I slowly released it as I turned around to walk off, only to turn back around as Kelsi called my name. "No matter what we go through or whether or not we get through this, I'll always love you and you're going to always be like a little sister to me."

I didn't even bother responding because no matter what, I would always love Kelsi, too, and I hated she was sucked into all this. Still, she was the one that brought it on herself.

Kelsi knew I was understanding and I would've been understanding had she come to me and told me about her and Rashad. As I stated, it was before me, so there was nothing I could do about it. If I stayed with him, it would've been on me. It would've been a choice I made. Not one they'd made for me.

Inside my truck, I pulled off as the tears I had been trying to hold in rolled down my face.

I texted Dyce on the way to Kelsi's house and asked what time he would be home so I could come over. I didn't tell him that I was headed to Kelsi's house because I didn't want to hear his mouth and I didn't need him to try to come with me. After the bullshit with Rashad following me, Dyce wanted to know my every move. I told him with all that, I could just share my location with him, but he didn't want that. He told me that he wasn't even that type of nigga, he just wanted a little communication so he could make sure I was okay.

I felt where he was coming from, but at the same time, I had no problem with sharing my location with him. Most times I was in the hotel room, waiting for him, anyway.

"What's up? You still in the room?" Dyce called me instead of texting me back. When I told him that I had left to go get myself something to eat, he said, "I'm about to pull up at the house. Come get me so we can go together."

I was hesitant to tell him okay, but I went on. The closer I got to his house, the more nervous I became about him seeing the truck. The last thing I wanted was for him to think I was being careless. He had just gotten the truck for me, and that bitch had already fucked it up. It was minor, but still...

Pulling up to his house, I pulled into the driveway behind his truck and got out. He kept his other two cars parked in the garage, being that he barely drove them. I got out and headed up to the front door and knocked. I heard his dogs barking and rolled my eyes. No matter how many times I came over here, I still wasn't used to them.

"What's up, Shawty?" Dyce asked as he pulled me in for a hug. His dogs were standing behind him, but when they saw it was me, they slowly walked off. I guess they had to make sure I wasn't here to harm him.

Since I had been spending more time with Dyce, he had been taking me to the backyard where his dogs were so I could watch him feed them. He said he wanted them to see me and get familiar with me since I was going to be around. That was understandable because his damn dogs didn't play about him.

"So, what's up? You good?" Dyce asked me once we were inside and he had closed and locked his front door.

"Yup... Hungry as hell."

"What you wanna eat?"

"I don't even know... Anything." I told him. He nodded his head up and down as his dog walked over to me. I tensed up and called his name. "Dyce...."

"Aye, King!" Dyce's deep voice caused him to turn around and head the other way. I guess since we weren't planning on staying long, he wasn't taking them to the backyard as he always did when I was here. "You ready?"

"Yeah..." I answered but didn't bother getting up from the couch. He noticed I was still sitting and asked me what was wrong. "I have to tell you something before we leave."

"What?" Dyce lifted a brow as he stared at me. I pushed the corner of my bottom lip into my mouth and said nothing. "That nigga been fucking with you again?"

"No... Hell, no!" I answered him quickly. He asked me, again, what was up as he took a seat on the arm of the chair across from me. "I went to Beauti's parent's house to talk to them. I told you how she been asking me to call her. So, I did, and she asked me to come by. I didn't want to at first, but I felt bad for not at least hearing her out. I went over there, and Beauti came while I was there."

"Word?" He looked eager to hear what happened next.

"Yeah, and I beat her ass!" Dyce pushed a smile on his face like he was proud of me.

"Wait a minute... Now, did you really beat her ass, or did you just get a good hit in, and think you won the fight?"

"No, I beat her ass... Like, literally, I scrubbed the ground with her ass."

"Damn... That's what's up right there!" Standing to his feet, he pulled me up and wrapped his arms around me, lifting me off the floor. My arms draped around his neck as my legs locked around his body while he spun us around. When he stopped, he said, "That bitch deserved that shit!"

"I know, right? I'ma beat her ass every time I see her until I get tired of doing it, and it's not even about Rashad. It's about her playing in my fucking face."

"We're about to go celebrate this shit!" He kissed me.

I laughed at his antics. "Hold on. What are we celebrating?"

"You beating her ass! She deserved that shit, and I know you proud as fuck about that W. That's why you told me."

"Uh, no... That's not why I told you." I released a soft chuckle before turning serious. When Dyce saw how serious I was, he slowly put me down and asked what was up. His eyes were narrowed like he was trying to read through me. "Don't get mad, but her crazy ass threw a rock and cracked my back window. I'll get it fixed, though. I promise I will."

"What?"

Dyce was wearing an expression on his face that I couldn't tell if it was because he was upset or just stressed the hell out from all my bullshit.

Saying nothing, he turned around and walked off with me slowly following. Being that he could only see the driver's side, I told him it was the back passenger window that was damaged. When he got around to that side, he ran his hand over the small crack where Beauti had thrown the rock.

"It's not that bad." He told me, still examining it. "It'll be fixed tomorrow." Dyce then hiked up his pants as he turned to me and asked what time I was going to be ready to go out.

I frowned at how understanding he was. "So, you're not mad?"

"Hell, no. I mean, that's what bitches do when they lose a fight. They try to damage shit. I'm surprised this was the only thing she did." I chuckled as I nodded my head up and down in agreement. I was surprised, yet, happy that Beauti didn't do much to my truck. Picking me up, Dyce threw me over his shoulder and walked us inside with me laughing.

Once in the house, he put me down and then headed to the back, calling his dogs, King and Queen. I followed behind him as the dogs took off running to the back door, already knowing it was time for them to go outside. Dyce had me pouring their dog food while he got their water.

Even with him in the cage with me, I was so damn scared. I had heard all about dogs attacking people and I wasn't trying to be attacked by these big ass dogs. However, Dyce said I had to learn how to feed his babies for when he wasn't home, and I had to do it.

I rolled my eyes at that because I damn sure wasn't trying to be out here feeding any damn dogs, but if I had to, I damn sure would.

"We're staying here tonight. You need to go back to the hotel and get something?" Dyce asked me as we walked back up to the house. I told him that I didn't, being that he insisted on me buying clothes and other things I needed to keep at his house.

If I didn't know any better, I would think he was trying to get me to move in with him. If he was, it would've been strange being that he had just paid for my room. I really hated Dyce had to do that for me, and it had me wanting to ask him if I could move in with him until I started getting my check from school or I got a job —whichever one came first.

I had still been filling out job applications, but I hadn't had any luck. One place had called me, and I had to do an interview last week, but I still hadn't heard from them yet. It had gotten to the point where I asked Dyce if he would hire me.

I didn't know if he thought I was playing or what, but after laughing in my face, he asked me how it would look if he hired me to work for him. I got where he was coming from, but something was going to have to give. This shit, being broke, wasn't the business.

Upstairs, we showered together and had a little sex session, then got dressed and headed out. We rode in his Bugatti—which I loved. Of course, I had never in my life been in one before, and I loved that Dyce was showing me to new things.

Pulling up to the nice upscale restaurant, the person working valet parked the car as we walked in. Dyce said his name and in no time, we were escorted to our seats.

"Bae, this place is nice," I told Dyce as I slid into the round booth. "I've never even heard of this place."

"Yeah, it's kind of new. I think it's been open for like a year now, or almost a year. It's my homeboy spot."

"Oh, okay…" After ordering our drinks, which were alcoholic

beverages, we made small talk until the waitress brought them to us. When she did, we ordered our food then sipped on our drinks, and took the three shots apiece that Dyce had ordered for us. I told him, "Let me find out you're trying to get me drunk on the low."

"Maybe..." He stretched his neck and buried his head in the crook of my neck, placing soft kisses there, causing me to squirm in my seat as my body quivered.

"Dyceeee." I groaned as I wrapped my arms around his neck, palming the back of his head with my hand. Although Rashad was affectionate, it was just something about Dyce being that way with me. We remain being touchy feeling until our food arrived.

I got the surprise of my life when Rashad walked in. Dyce was stuffing his face, so I was the one that noticed him first.

"Dyce... Don't look up yet, but Rashad just walked in." He did the opposite of what I said and looked dead up and into Rashad's face. He had already spotted us and was looking our way.

I looked from him to Dyce and the fact that Dyce had leaned back and was now wearing a cocky smirk on his face had me shaking my head. I didn't know if it was because of Rashad's presence or the woman he had with him. It was Dyce's ex, which confused the hell out of me, being that Beauti was just fighting over him and accusing me of being jealous that he was *her* husband.

"When the hell did they start dating?" I mumbled.

"I don't even know, but I'm glad. Now she can leave me the hell alone."

"Oh, she was going to have to do that anyway, because It's not happening." Those words left my mouth without my consent, but I didn't regret them. I had no plans of letting this seemingly good man go. I just prayed those exact words didn't come back and bite me in the ass.

Dyce looked over at me and licked his lips before tucking the bottom one between his teeth. He was still wearing the cocky smirk, but I was looking at his ass with a serious expression, letting him know I meant those words.

"Is that right?" He finally said.

I leaned over to him, looking up as I said, "You damn right!"

The smile on his face widened so much that he showed all thirty-two teeth before he leaned in and kissed me. Now, I didn't know whose tongue eased into whose mouth first, but we ended up sharing a much needed passionate kiss. It was hungrily. Sloppy and anything else you could think of.

I didn't know about Dyce, but I was happy that my ex was seeing this and there was no doubt in my mind that he was looking. I just felt it, and I was right, too. When me and Dyce parted, out of the corner of my eyes I could see not only Rashad but Dyce's ex mugging the shit out of us.

After we finished eating, we sat around laughing and drinking. I was so tipsy that after the last shot he ordered; I had to tell him that I was done. He knew I was drunk, too, because I wasn't doing a good job at whispering what I was going to do to him when we got back to his house or what I wanted him to do to me.

I was even caressing his dick underneath the table.

Our interaction was cut short by the sound of a throat being cleared. When we both turned to look in the direction it had come from, I wasted no time shifting in my seat as I looked over at Dyce. He was staring directly at Rashad, who thought it was a bright idea to come over to our table.

Just as I turned back to face him and I opened my mouth to speak, Dyce spoke up. "What the fuck you want, nigga?" He spoke with much venom laced in his voice, and the unpleasant look on his face had me scared and I hadn't done shit.

Rashad didn't pay him any attention as his eyes never left me. "Nique, can I talk to you?"

"Nigga…" Since knowing Dyce, I had never seen him move so

fast. Him sliding out of the booth and snatching Rashad up happened so fast that neither of us saw it coming.

"Dyce!" By the time I was able to get out of the booth, Dyce had spun Rashad around and had him in a chokehold position. I could see on Rashad's face that he was fighting for his life in that short time. Pulling at Dyce's arm as bystanders watched in shock and some even let out gasps, I begged him to let Rashad go. We were in a public place, and I didn't want Dyce killing this man.

Rashad wasn't worth it.

"Dyce, I'm begging you. Please don't do this."

"Dyce, what the fuck? Let him go!" His ex that happened to have been Rashad's date at the time, made her way over to us and was now pulling on Dyce's arm as well. I wanted to push her ass away from him and tell her not to touch him, but right now, I needed all the help I could get before Dyce killed this man.

"Nigga, I don't know what the fuck you thought this was, but don't you ever disrespect me? I'll fucking kill yo' bitch ass! Now get the fuck away from our table!" Dyce released Rashad, causing him to immediately start coughing from nearly being choked to death.

"Damn, Dyce… That shit wasn't even called for. All he wanted to do was talk to her."

"Bitch, he didn't even have a reason to come over here, period. Shad knows I don't fuck with him, so he wanted to be messy as fuck and got what he deserved." I meant that. No, I didn't want Dyce to kill him, being that we were surrounded by a lot of people, but at the same time, what in the hell did Rashad expect would happen? What he did was disrespectful as hell, like Dyce said, and he was lucky I was here to stop him from meeting his maker.

"Bitch?" She looked at me like I was crazy. "Ain't you the same bitch that had a problem with me calling you that? You and this nigga, both, had a problem with it, but now it's okay for you to call me one?"

"Aye, what's going on? Dyce, you good?" A guy walked up

dressed in a nice black suede suit asked. He had dreads that were pulled up in a man bun with the sides cut low. He was a nice looking light-skinned guy and, being that he knew Dyce, I suspected he was the owner.

"Yeah, I'm good. Just about to snap a mothafucka's neck if he doesn't get the fuck away from me."

By now, Rashad had his coughs under control and was mugging the shit out of Dyce as if he was contemplating his next move. I could see in his eyes that he didn't at all appreciate what had gone down, but again, what in the hell did he expect?

Not even giving a fuck, Dyce stepped in his face and said, "Nigga, you got your nostrils flared like you wanna do something?"

"Dyce, come on, now." I pulled at his arms. At this point, Dyce was just being a bully. I loved it but at the same time, as bad as I didn't want to, I felt sorry for Rashad. I knew this shit had to have been embarrassing for him and I hated that my heart cared enough to not want him to be humiliated. Even so, I said, "Let's just go, babe. You already know he's not worth this shit."

"Yeah, bruh." The guy that clearly knew Dyce stepped into the small space that separated Dyce and Rashad. He was facing Dyce and spoke in a low tone when he tried reasoning with him. "This shit ain't worth it. You know you can't kill buddy like this… Not in front of all these mothafuckas. So, just take your lady and go home. Sleep this shit off or something. You don't even have to worry about your tab. Everything's on the house."

He put us out of his establishment in a nice way, which was understandable being that Dyce was showing his black ass. While he and Rashad continue giving each other a stare-down, I grabbed my purse off the table and was ready to go.

"Dyce, you wrong as hell for this!"

"Fuck you, Jordyn!" Dyce grabbed my hand and pulled me in front of him. I walked off, not even bothering to give Rashad a second look. Nevertheless, I felt his eyes piercing a hole through my soul as I walked by him. Before we could make it out of earshot, we heard the owner tell Rashad and his date that once they paid their tab and had their food boxed up, they could leave.

The fact that they still had to pay was funny to me and I knew it was one more thing to piss them off.

Outside, neither me nor Dyce said a word until we got in the car. Dyce was the first to speak up as he pulled off like a bat out of hell. He reached over and turned the radio down and told me, "You know I'ma fuck around and kill that nigga, right?"

I didn't say anything because honestly; I didn't know what to say. I was still replaying the whole scene in my head. It was something from a movie. Never in a million years would I have imagined my life to be this drama filled. Hell, to have any type of drama and it made me wonder, had I not gone to prison, would all this be happening?

I'd always heard, everything happened for a reason. Maybe I wouldn't have met Dyce if I wouldn't have gotten locked up. I didn't know. Everything that was happening was just crazy, to say the least.

"Straight up, Nique... I'm about to ask you something and I want you to be honest with me. I'm going to ask you one time and only this time... Do you still want to be with that nigga?"

"What?" My face contorted into a frown. "Hell no, I don't want to be with him. I mean, of course, I still care a little about his well-being, but that shit is natural. I can guarantee you that you don't want nothing to happen to your—"

"I don't give a fuck about nobody that I'm no longer in a relationship with!" He cut me off. "I guess I'm not going to sit up here like I don't get what you're saying, though. It took me a while to completely get over my exes, but our shit was different. Neither one of them had no babies on a nigga or married someone else."

"Okay, yeah, Shad did me dirty, but this was a nigga I had been with for ten years, Dyce. My feelings for him—"

"And it should be the same reason you don't give a fuck about me killing him. You were with him for ten years, and he married some other bitch and started a family with her. Let me ask you this; how you feel about your homegirl? Do you care about her well-being?" I couldn't even answer that.

When all this first came to light, I thought I was going to still have love for Beauti, but as the days went by, my hate for her only grew. Yes, I knew it was crazy for me to still care for Rashad's well-being, but in my heart, I knew it was more so of me looking out for Dyce in this situation. That overpowered any amount of care I had in my heart for Rashad.

Yet, I felt it was useless to tell him that. So, I just didn't say anything at all.

Seeing that I wasn't going to answer his question, Dyce let out a chuckle as he reached over and turned up the radio. For the rest of the ride back to his house, neither of us said a word as we got lost in our thoughts.

12

THE WRONG ONE!

Rashad Russell

The fact that I couldn't enjoy fucking Jordyn's brains out for thinking about Unique had me pissed the fuck off. It was my first time having sex with her and I was supposed to have been making a good impression. Instead, I was thinking about my ex and that big ass nigga.

I didn't know if Dyce thought I was a sucker or what, but I was really getting sick of his disrespect.

I couldn't believe he had snatched me up like I was his bitch, in front of Unique, but in front of Jordyn as well. Had it not been for Unique interfering, one of us would've been dead.

I had been trying my best to stay out of the nigga's way when I should've been gunning for his head, but I had a lot of shit going on, dealing with Beauti's ass.

My mind was made up and first thing in the morning, I was going to go ahead and file for a divorce. Even if Unique didn't take me back, I wasn't staying married to her. Not at all did I regret my kids, but after losing Unique, it made me regret that I ever started fucking with Beauti.

It was crazy because I used to sit and think about myself fucking not only Beauti and Unique, but Kelsi, too, though it was only one time with her. That shit still had a nigga feeling good as fuck about it, and the fact that Kelsi had kept it a secret for all these years had my ass feeling bad for telling her sister. In my defense, at the time, I didn't know my wife was going to go back and run her mouth. Her using that to have her sister agree to witness us getting married was what I would've never expected her to do.

However, when she told me that she was able to get Kelsi to agree to it as she gave me a conniving grin, I knew what was up.

I didn't care, though. I just wanted to marry Beauti. Not only was she pregnant by me and I thought it was the right thing to do, but then, I thought I loved her more than Unique and I thought I wanted to spend the rest of my life with her.

My doubts started kicking in when Unique got out and I realized I was still in love with her and couldn't let her go. Don't get shit twisted; I still had plenty of love for Beauti. She just wasn't the one I wanted to be with.

I wanted Unique and her only, but if she really aborted my baby, then I knew there were no chances of me getting her back, and that shit was slowly killing a nigga.

"Are you okay?" The sound of Jordyn's voice snapped me from my thoughts. I had so much on my mind that I had pretty much blacked out of what was going on at the moment. My body was numbed and though I thought I was beating the pussy, I didn't feel shit.

We were in a missionary position with her legs wrapped around my back and her arms draped around my neck. When my movement came to a halt, we just stared down at one another.

"You good?" She asked me again as she rubbed me on the

back. Jordyn had so much concern in her eyes, and I hated all this had happened in front of her, especially when that nigga was her ex. As soon as we got to the restaurant and I saw Unique sitting not too far from me, I told Jordyn that she was my ex. I didn't tell her that she was my wife's best friend, though, because then I would have to inform her of my griminess and the last thing I wanted was for her to see me in a different light.

Bad enough, I had a wife and was here with her.

Rolling off her, I laid flat on the side of her as I let out a heavy sigh while running my hand down my face. "Man, I just want to apologize about the shit that went down tonight. I wasn't trying to disrespect you or no shit like that, I just wanted to talk to her about something important."

I was trying to see if she had really aborted my child because if she hadn't, we had to discuss what to expect with the baby so she wouldn't be caught off guard like me and Beauti. She was being a bitch since she got with that nigga, and it was pissing me the fuck off. I had been trying to be patient, but there were only going to be so many times that nigga came at me wrong before I just said fuck what would happen to me and got at his ass.

As I've stated before, I didn't personally know Dyce, but I knew how deep he was in the streets. He had a lot of niggas that were willing to kill for his black ass, and I wasn't trying to die. I had kids to live for and I wanted to be here for them.

"You don't have to apologize to me." Was all Jordyn responded with before silence took over. It didn't last long, though. She turned on her side to face me, pushing up on her elbow and resting her face on her hand so that she could get a better look at me. I turned to face her and was met with a strange look. "So, you were cheating on your wife with her or something? I'm asking because, from the way you went over there, it was like the breakup is fresh between ya'll."

I ran my tongue over my suddenly dry lips before turning my

head away from her. I stared up at the ceiling, trying to see if I wanted to answer her question or not.

Jordyn and me had been talking on the phone and texting for a little over two weeks now and I was digging her. I had even come to her hotel and chilled with her, twice. We didn't have sex or no shit like that. We just got to know one another a little better, and it felt good to vent to her about Beauti. Jordyn knew I was unhappy in my marriage, and I had even told her that I only married Beauti because she told me that she was pregnant.

Don't get me wrong; I loved the fuck out of her, and I thought I wanted to spend the rest of my life with her, but if she wouldn't have been pregnant, I honestly didn't think I would've married her when I did. Well, I knew I wouldn't, but it was too late to dwell on the past. It'd happened and there wasn't a damn thing I could do about it.

After seeing I wasn't going to answer her, she climbed on me in a riding position, leaning down to kiss my lips before sitting back up.

I rubbed my hand up and down her butt before bringing them around to her front side, trailing them up to her perky breast. I pinched her nipples as I felt my dick swelling underneath her. Being that I had so much on my mind minutes ago, I was unable to get my nut and now I needed to release all the built-up stress I had in me.

My hands made their way to her back, and I tried pulling her down to me, but her body stiffened as she shook her head. "No, I wanna talk. You told me that you're staying the night with me, so we'll have all night to do whatever you want. Okay?" She was rubbing my chest the whole time she spoke, as her eyes never left mine.

I had no intentions of going back home and let her know that tonight, I was all hers. I couldn't even believe Jordyn didn't care that I was married, and I knew if her nosey ass grandma knew about us, she would have a fucking fit.

"Okay. What's up?"

"I want you to answer my question, but before you do, you know my grandma lives right across the hall from ya'll. She told me something went down, but I thought she was only assuming."

"What she tell you?" I wanted to know, already knowing. That's why I hated that old ass lady now, and her ass was happy I wasn't a killer because I would've been murked her old ass for telling Unique on my ass... Even though she was oblivious to what she was revealing.

"Well..." she sang. "She told me that your wife had introduced her to her friend, claiming the girl was her best friend or some shit, and the girl came over and she told her that you had taken her to the hospital to have the babies."

"What else?"

She shrugged. "Nothing really, but she thinks you were sleeping with your wife's best friend." I couldn't even make eye contact with her after that. I was ashamed to even tell her that it was true, I had been sleeping with best friends, but it was deeper than what her grandma knew. "Tell me... I wanna know everything, which it's quite obvious about what's been going on. That was the wife's friend, right?"

"Yeah, it was."

"And let me guess, she got tired of being the side chick and started fucking with my ex?" I just stared at her. "Shad, tell me what happened. Clearly, it's not like I'm going to go back and tell your wife or no shit like that. I would be a fool too and I'm laying up here with you. Plus, your wife is a bitch. So, I don't feel sorry for her ass, at all."

"Man, it's deeper than what your grandma told you... Just know that."

"What, you got her pregnant, too?" Again, I didn't say anything.

Only a frustrating sigh left my mouth, and she got the hint that I didn't want to talk about it. "Okay, fine. We don't have to talk about it. Just know, if you want to, I'm here." With that, she leaned down and kissed me.

The kiss was slow and precise as she rotated her midsection. Her wet pussy rubbing against my hard dick had me ready to fuck the shit out of her and this time, I was pushing Unique and that fat ass nigga to the back of my mind. This was a night that I want to enjoy with no interruptions.

∼

It was after three in the evening when I finally made it home. Beauti's car was parked in its usual space and, being that the parking lot was semi-empty, I was able to park right next to her.

Getting out, I slowly walked up the stairs and as I reached the front door, I took in a heavy breath and slowly released it as I unlocked it and walked in. The house was quiet. No babies crying, no TV playing, or nothing.

As always, I sat my key on the countertop and headed to the back of the house. The bathroom door was opened in me and Beauti's bedroom, letting me know she was in the shower. I looked in the bassinets and didn't see either of the kids, I didn't bother looking in their bedrooms being that we had yet to get them their baby beds and they wouldn't be sleeping in there anytime soon.

Plus, Beauti said she wanted to wait until she got a house to get them one and I was okay with that, though I knew if she got a house, I wouldn't be living with her or getting her one. I was over her and the fucking marriage at this gotdamn point.

After seeing that the twins weren't home, I stormed into the bathroom where the shower was still running. I snatched the curtains back, causing her to jump. "Where the fuck are my kids at, Beauti?"

"What?" Beauti scowled at me, letting me know that she didn't appreciate me coming in here questioning her about anything. After I asked her again with a lot more bass in my voice, she reached over and turned off the water. "Shad, you better get the fuck out my face right now. If you cared about your kids and their whereabouts, then you would've brought yo' ass home last night."

"Man, don't start that bullshit." I backed up some so that she could get out of the shower. As she wrapped the towel around her body, I said, "My fucking kids better not be at your mama's house when you wouldn't let me take them to mine yesterday."

"Boy, fuck you!" She walked past me. "Like I told you yesterday, fuck you and that bitch! My kids ain't going over there. Not until I can go, but to be honest with you, I don't even want to go no more. I never liked her ass anyway. Fuck her!"

"Man, you better watch yo' fucking mouth." Beauti's mouth was too gotdamn reckless, and she had a nigga ready to lay hands on her ass.

"Where the fuck you were last night, Shad? That hoes ass bitch jumped on me yesterday and then I get home and my fucking husband ain't here and wouldn't even answer the damn phone for me."

"What? Who jumped on you?" I asked, as my face frowned in concern.

"Who the hell do you think? That bitch, Nique. Then my parents let it happen. That's why I can't stand that hoe now. I swear I can't wait for her ass to go back to prison. Keep fucking with me; she'll be in there a lot longer than she was last time."

"What? Man, don't even say no foul ass shit like that."

She spun around so fast to face me. "Oh, you gon' cry if she goes back?" She had the nerve to look at me like she dared me to say I would. When I didn't say anything, she added, "If you are, then you might as well cry now because she'll be back in there as soon as the police catch her ass."

"Man..." I sang as I shook my head and walked out of the room. I didn't even want to hear that bullshit.

Instead of just leaving like the little voice in the back of my mind was telling me to, I walked over to the couch and flopped down on it. I wanted to come home and relax and Beauti was fucking that up for me. When I left Jordyn this morning, I got up with Don so we could count, and that shit felt good. Since all this bullshit happened with Unique, I had been neglecting my responsibilities in the streets and as a boss. I had kids, and I had to get back to the money so that I could take care of them.

The last thing I wanted or needed was for Don to think I was slacking and start working with another mothafucka.

"So, you just going to walk off on me like that? I bet you won't do Nique's ass like that. You used to kiss her ass because you didn't want her mad at you. I'm your wife! Why can't I get the same treatment?" I didn't even pay Beauti's ass no attention as she walked over to the couch where I was. She stood over me like I was a child, causing me to power off my phone and put it up before she tried to grab it. Then her feelings were going to be really hurt. "Say, nigga! You married me and been treating me like the side hoe since she came home. I should've listened to my sister when she said you weren't shit instead of thinking she was being jealous."

"I guess you should've then!" I told her as I got up, bumping into her with so much force that she fell over on the loveseat. She was up and rushing over to me as I walked over to the counter to grab my keys to leave. I damn sure wasn't trying to stay and argue with her as. "You need to be going wherever the fuck my kids at and get them."

"You need to kiss my ass!" Beauti tried to grab my keys from me, but I pushed her back and asked her what the fuck she was doing, which was obvious. "You think you slick, but I know what you trying to do. You trying to get that bitch Nique back. That's why you won't let me and your kids move into that house, but guess what, nigga, that bitch won't be living in it either when I get done with her. Just like I got her ass locked up the first time, I'm getting her locked up again."

"What the fuck did you just say?" I just knew I had to have been hearing her wrong, and she didn't just confess to me that she was the reason Unique got locked up. With a shake of my head, I told her, "I know you didn't just say what the fuck I think you said."

"I damn sure did!"

"So, you had Nique locked up?" The look on her face said it all and before she knew it, I was in her face, grabbing her by the neck and slamming her ass on the floor, causing her to scream. "Bitch, are you fucking crazy?"

"Shad, what the fuck?" Beauti jumped up. "Really, nigga? You hit me because of her, and the bitch doesn't even want you? Now I'm really glad I went and pressed charges on her ass, and when she gets locked up and serves the rest of her probation time in prison, I bet you be back over here with your family. I can't wait for that hoe's probation officer to get word that she has a warrant for her arrest, since it seems reporting her ass for staying out past curfew ain't working."

I backed handed her before I knew it, but I didn't regret it. Before she could even fall over, I snatched her up by her hair and dragged her by the couch, ignoring her screaming for me to let her go.

"Bitch, what the fuck were you even thinking? You stupid bitch!" I backhanded her ass again before tossing her onto the couch. She rolled off it and tried scooting away from me, but I wasn't having that. She had so much to say seconds ago but now she was on mute. "While you're so worried about Nique and taking a warrant out on her, you need to be worried about the divorce papers your mothafuckin' ass will be getting soon."

"What?" She did like she was about to get up, but I mushed her ass right back down. I was so tempted to punch her ass that I didn't know what to do. I had never in my life been so mad before, but Beauti, my soon-to-be ex-wife had crossed the fucking line.

After all the shit we had done to Unique, for her to try to have the girl locked back up was fucking insane. She was hitting below the belt with that one. I couldn't even believe she was the reason Unique had gone to jail in the first place.

A part of me felt Beauti was lying being that Unique had taken the charge for me, but if she was lying, my heart believed she damn sure had something to do with it, and fucking with Unique was fucking with the wrong one.

13

DEAD TO ME!

Dyce Walker

I had been trying my best to not think about what had gone down two days ago at my homeboy's restaurant, but that shit was hard to do. My anger wasn't even toward Unique, not anymore, because I guess I should've been considerate of her feelings. I just didn't get how she still cared what happened to that nigga after what he had done to her, but after some much needed thinking and me talking to my sister about the situation, I realized it wasn't as easy for some women to let go as others.

My sister told me to just be patient with Unique and in due time, she will no longer give a fuck about that nigga. I knew she eventually wouldn't, but it still fucked my head up that it seemed anything I did to the bitch ass nigga she had a problem with it. Even so, my sister called herself, checking me, telling me to keep my black ass out of it, but that was hard to do when a woman that had stolen my heart was involved.

As I drove to my bar after leaving my sister's house, I called Unique to let her know that I was stopping by my spot and then going to the hotel where she was. Tonight, I was going to ask her to move in with me. Shit, might as well. Since she had moved out of the house with that nigga, we were damn near inseparable.

She couldn't get enough of me and I damn sure couldn't get enough of her.

Just as I put my phone back in the cup holder, it started vibrating again. When I picked it up, I saw it was Angie and frowned. It wasn't a frown like she had no business calling me, because since I had started fucking with Unique and we found out that she was her probation officer, Angie had called me a few times.

So, this frown was me wondering what in the hell was going on now.

All I could think about was that Rashad's bitch ass had been calling back up to the office to report Unique. Just the thought of it had me pissed before I could even hit send and answer the phone for her.

"Yeah? What's up, Angie?" I answered.

"Hey, Dyce. Are you home?" I instantly picked up on her voice and knew something was wrong. My antennas went up as I told her that I wasn't home and asked her again, what was up. She released a heavy sigh as she responded. "I need to talk to you about something, and this can't be discussed over the phone."

"I can come by ya'll crib if you want me to."

"No!" She damn near shouted. "We can meet somewhere else, and I have to pick my kids up from daycare in two hours. So—"

"A'ight. I'm on my way to the bar. You can meet me there." When she said okay, we ended the call. The whole ride there, I wondered what in the hell was going on and why she didn't want me to meet her at her and my brother's house just like any other time, but I didn't give it much thought, knowing it was probably nothing.

When I made it to my spot, I immediately spotted Angie's car.

She wasn't inside when I passed it to get to my assigned spot in front of the door. Getting out, I walked inside to find her sitting at the bar, throwing back a shot. I spoke to a few customers and employers as I made my way over to her and spoke. She looked stressed the fuck out and like she had been crying. Her eyes were puffy and red.

"You good?" I had never seen my sister-in-law like this and was concerned like a mothafucka.

"Not really. I'm divorcing your brother, and I need to talk to you about his ass." My head jerked back as I frown in confusion when those words rushed out her mouth. Her and my brother had always had the perfect relationship to me. So, hearing her state she was divorcing him had me scratching my head, wondering where in the hell that had come from. Before I could ask her, she added, "He's been on some bullshit, and I really need to talk to you about it, Dyce."

"Do you want to talk here, or—"

"Nah, we can go up to my office. Come on." I turned around and walked off, knowing she would follow. All I wanted to do was know what in the hell my brother had done that was so bad she was divorcing his ass. Tony wasn't a cheater as far as I knew, and he had always been about his family. So, this shit confused me.

Inside my office, I closed the door when Angie walked inside. While she walked over to the couch, I took a seat on the edge of my desk, facing her as I gave her my undivided attention.

Neither of us said a word as her chest heaved up and caved back in from the loud ass sigh, she released. Then, she hit me with, "Tony has been cheating on me, and this ain't the first time."

"What?"

Nodding her head up and down, she continued with, "Yes. It first happened with someone that worked with him, and when I should've left him, he guilt me into staying, telling me that I was busy with school and work and didn't have time for him. I knew I would be done with school soon, so I decided to stay and balance my time between him, school and work. Now I wished I would've just left his ass and let that bitch deal with him."

"Are you sure?" I folded my arms across my chest, still finding it hard to believe my brother was a cheater. "I've never known Tony to cheat on you, Angie."

"Tony is conniving and sneaky as fuck!" She rolled her eyes as she sipped her drink. All I could do was shake my head as I stared at her. None of this was making sense to me, but he was her husband, and I knew she wouldn't lie about something like that. Even so, I had already made a mental note to call him once I was done with her. Not saying a word, she sat her glass down on the table in front of her and grabbed her purse.

I know damn well she doesn't have no fucking proof. I thought as I watched her pull out a stack of papers. Her purse was big as hell, the reason I didn't know she had them.

"Aye, I don't need you to prove shit to me, I believe—" She cut me off by walking over to me and telling me to take the papers she was holding. I was hesitant to get them because I didn't think it was that serious for her to show me proof that he was cheating.

"You'll want to see this, Dyce." I watched as her eyes became glossy and that shit worried me. It had me reluctantly taking the papers from her and looking at them. Curiosity had gotten the best of me, anyway, because now I wanted to know what in the hell was on these papers that she wanted me to see so bad.

When I had them in my hand, I saw that they were text messages between him and a number that I didn't recognize. I frowned as I read the first couple of messages. The last thing I wanted to see was my brother talking about fucking someone else. However, it was one that caught my eye, causing me to look over at Angie, who had made her way back over to the couch. She was sitting her drink down as tears rolled down her face.

"That nigga had kids on you?" I shockingly asked.

"According to those messages he does, but he claim he doesn't know for sure if they're his or not."

"He claim he doesn't know?" I repeated. "Why won't he get a test done for them?"

"Because his ass is scared, they're going to come back his. Like, the nigga could possibly have twins out here."

All I could do was shake my head. This shit was crazy, and the messages said he damn sure knew they were his and was trying to keep it from his wife. As I continue scanning over them, I had to chuckle to myself because whoever the bitch was, she had my brother's balls in her hands. She was blackmailing him like a mothafucka, threatening to tell Angie if he didn't oblige by her rules.

"What the fuck?" Those words rolled off my tongue in a mumble.

I guess from the way my facial expression had changed from shock to mad, Angie somewhat knew what part of the messages I was on because she spoke up and said, "I wanted to show you sooner, but I had to process all this bullshit."

"This that bitch, Beauti he's fucking with?" It didn't take a rocket scientist to figure that out with the way Unique's name was mentioned in these texts between her and my brother.

"Yeah, and he's been creeping with her off and on for years. He told me that much when I confronted him about these messages." She paused, shaking her head. I didn't even want to read any more of the bullshit because I had already read enough. The fact that my brother had been behind all this bullshit when it came to Unique had me ready to kill his ass. "Dyce, I didn't know any of this. I had a feeling he was cheating again, and I was able to hack into his phone records and pull up his text messages. I would've never guessed he would do something as sneaky as this. I guess I should've known, though, because he had a lot to say about you being with her and how he didn't think it was a good idea. I just figured it was because she had been in prison."

I was pissed and I didn't want to hear the shit she had to say. No, I didn't believe Angie knew about this for the simple fact that she brought the shit to my attention. It was all my brother, and Angie was right; it was exactly why he had so much to say.

He was against us because his ass was trying to send her back to prison.

"Where the fuck Tony at?" I asked Angie. When she told me that he was home and tried to utter something else, I walked off without hearing shit else she said. Paying his ass a visit was the only thing that was on my mind.

"Dyce, where you going?" I was walking out of my office without saying shit else to Angie. Before I could make it downstairs, she was rushing down them, telling me to wait. Once we were outside, she asked me if I was going to her house where Tony was, and again, I didn't say shit and she could tell by my facial expression that I was pissed the fuck off and she needed to let me be.

Inside my car, I headed straight to my brother's house, with Angie trailing behind me. She got out before I could and rushed over to where I was.

"Dyce, please don't throw away your freedom over this bullshit. It's not worth it." She tried reasoning with me, already knowing I didn't play about Unique. If anybody knew how I felt about Unique, it was definitely my sister-in-law... Her and that nigga, Shad.

Ignoring her, I walked up to the porch just as the front door was opening. My rage went up a notch just as I laid eyes on my brother. I grabbed his ass, snatching him out the door and throwing him up against the house.

"Yo, what the fuck?" Tony shouted as his hand went up to grab me only for him to stop in his tracks and look past me. Angie calling my name caused him to look at her and then back at me. His whole posture changed, showing that he already knew what was up.

I was so hurt right now that I didn't even know what to say. All I could do was glare at him. I hated the thought of killing my brother, but the shit was wrong with what he had been doing. Unique hadn't done shit to him, and for him to team up with that busted bitch to try to have her locked back up was foul as fuck...

"Dyce, bro..." My hand shot up around his neck. I squeezed with all my might until I felt he was losing consciousness, ignoring Angie telling me that I was killing him. I didn't let go until I was good and gotdamn ready to. As he doubled over, holding his neck, I brought my knee up and kneed his ass, causing him to fall to the ground. "Ahhhh, fuck!"

I didn't feel sorry for his ass and was tempted to stomp him while he was down there. Angie didn't feel sorry for him, either, because she didn't bother to make sure he was okay. She stood behind me, still telling me that my brother wasn't worth it. She got in my head though, when she told me that Unique needed me and I wouldn't do her no good locked up. I knew then that I needed to back off and leave the house before I ended up fucking Tony up for real.

"You fucking told him when I asked you to keep it between us?" Although Tony coughs those words out, I heard him loud and clear. I stopped in my tracks and turned back around to face him.

"You fucking right, she told me!" I walked back up on him, getting all in his bloody ass face. His nose was bleeding so bad from when I kneed him. "Pussy ass nigga, I should've known something was up when you had so much to say about her. You a fucking bitch ass nigga and if you weren't my brother, I'll murk yo' ass right now."

"Man, Dyce... Her homegirl was threatening to tell my wife about us. I couldn't afford to lose my family."

"So you try to send an innocent woman back to prison." He dropped his head. "You a bitch ass nigga for that shit, Tony."

"I know man, and I wanted to tell you what her homegirl was up to, but come on, bruh... You know how much I loved my—"

"You better not say you love me because it's a fucking lie if you do!" Angie cut him off, not wanting to hear shit he had to say, and I didn't blame her. I would've never guessed my brother would be this low down. While a part of me felt like a dumb ass for going to Rashad's house and accusing him of calling Unique's probation officer on her, the other part still felt he deserve the little damage I had done to his face. "If you loved me, none of this bullshit would be happening."

"Ang, I do... I told you, I fucked up, baby." Tony reached out to grab Angie, but she quickly smacked his hand away, telling him not to touch her. "Man, what the fuck was I supposed to do? The bitch was threatening to tell you about me and her and I couldn't let you down a second time. Not only that but Dyce..."

I cocked a brow as he looked my way, giving him a look that spoke a million words. I couldn't voice enough how much I wanted to kill my own blood brother. As I narrowed my eyes, I waited for him to say whatever it was he had to say.

"When she first came to me about calling my wife's job to report Nique, I told her no because it was too risky, but then the dumb ass girl called my job and lied on me and almost got me fired."

"What?" By the way Angie said that, I knew it was the first time she had heard about that.

Tony ignored her, as his eyes never left me. "The mothafucka started investigating me, asking me all types of shit that I didn't even know about. When Beauti told me that she had something to do with it, I knew I had to step up and do what she wanted. Bruh, I'm sorry, man... And you're right. That's why I didn't want you with her because I knew —"

"Because you knew the file shit you were on..." Angie's words trailed off. I was over this shit and didn't want to hear nothing else his bitch ass had to say.

Releasing a heavy breath, I told him straight up, "Listen, I can't rock with no grimy ass mothafucka like you. I don't give a fuck what you and that hoe got going on, but leave Unique the fuck out of it. This is your only warning and the only reason you're getting that is because you're my brother." Hiking up my pants, I closed in the small gap that separated us and I added, "There won't be another warning, and I put that on my life."

With that, I turned around and walked off, passing Angie. My brother called my name, but I ignored him. The nigga was dead to me at this point. Some might've felt like I was choosing Unique over my own flesh and blood, and a nigga was. Yeah, I knew blood was thicker than water. In this case, it wasn't. My brother had done the ultimate no-no, and it went deeper than Unique being with me. He was grimy and should have taken his infidelities like a fucking man.

He had shown his hand and with the games, he was playing; I didn't even know if I could trust his ass or not.

Inside my car, I started my engine but didn't pull off right away. I waited around as Angie and him argued because I didn't want to leave her there with him. When she was able to get inside her car and pull off, I did as well.

So much shit was on my mind that I couldn't even go back to Unique's hotel. How in the fuck was I going to face her after all this shit? I knew I was going to eventually have to tell her what was up, but it just wasn't going to be right now.

14

WHEN KARMA HITS!

Beauti Woods-Russell

I had been home for two days because I was too embarrassed to leave. I couldn't even go pick my kids up from my parent's house because I didn't want anyone to see the damage Rashad, my husband, had done to my face. I had a bruise on the left side of it, a swollen and busted lip, and a cut over my right eye, causing it to be swollen.

Every time I looked in the mirror, I just got depressed. Rashad had never put his hands on me before. Not even on Unique when they were together. The side he showed me the other day was one that I didn't even know lived within him. It scared me but pissed me off at the same time because of the reason behind it.

I had not only called this man a bitch, but his mama as well. That wasn't what triggered him, though. It was me talking shit about Unique. Then the bastard hadn't even come home or at least called to apologize to me. Haven't even called to check on his kids. I was fed the fuck up because I didn't deserve this.

As bad as I didn't want to admit it, I was starting to see things for what they really were and would always be. My sister was right; Rashad would never put me before Unique and now I felt like a fool for thinking he would. Now I felt alone and lost. I'd chosen love over my family and my best friend. Now it had come back and bit me in the ass.

Even so, I still wasn't ready to give up on my marriage... on my husband.

I loved Rashad with my whole soul, and nothing would ever change that. We were a family and when he found out that I was pregnant; he was so excited and told me that he always dreamed of having a family. No, he didn't stay with me but being that I was carrying his kids and he was talking to me, what else was I to think? At this point, I just didn't know if he really meant it.

None of this was making sense to me and as bad as I wanted to believe my husband would come back to his senses, my heart didn't think so. I was miserable with the way my life was turning out. The last thing I wanted was to be a single parent. Besides me loving Rashad with every fiber I had in me, the other reason I wanted to marry him was because I didn't want to be a single parent.

Releasing a heavy sigh as I stared at myself in the mirror, I shook my head before turning around and heading to the door. I was disgusted at the reflection staring back at me. My face was still black and blue from the beating I'd endured the other day by the hands of my husband, and it made me hate that I loved him so much and didn't call the cops on his ass.

The same way I had pressed charges on Unique, I should've done the same on my husband. Little did he know, though, I had pictures in my phone of the damage he had done to my face and if he didn't come back to me, I was going straight to the police.

Not bothering to put on any make-up or shades to cover my face, I grabbed my keys and walked straight out my front door. As I was walking down the stairs, I met Mrs. Sally's granddaughter walking up to them. When she saw me, she stopped, and her eyes bucked as she looked into my face. I gave her a, *what the fuck you looking at*, look.

"Are you okay?" She asked me.

With a suck of my teeth, I told her ass, "Girl, get the fuck out my business." With that, I walked right past her. We weren't friends, and there was no reason for her to act as if we were. It was just something about her ass that I didn't like.

Inside my car, I headed out of the apartment complex and drove straight to my sister's house. A conversation with her was long overdue. I know, I know, I should've been going to my parent's house to see my kids, but I felt I had plenty of time to do that. Right now, I wanted to apologize to my sister and finally let her know that she was right about Rashad.

When I pulled up to her house, I was relieved to only see her car parked in the driveway. Getting out, I walked up to the front door. Just as I was getting ready to knock, the door opened, and I was face-to-face with Kelsi and another woman. The woman pushed a smile onto her face and spoke. I didn't bother speaking back because I was too busy looking at my sister. She had her eyes locked on me as well.

I couldn't read her expression. So, I didn't know if she was wondering what I was doing at her house after the last time I saw her, or if she felt some type of sympathy for me. After all, it was obvious something had happened to me by my face, and Unique didn't do it.

"Can I talk to you, Kels?" I asked in a hushed tone. She pressed her lips together as she moved to the side to let me in. When I walked in, I saw all her nail supplies out and knew the woman that had just left was a customer. Not bothering to sit down, I turned to face her as she was asking what happened to my face. I didn't come flat out and tell her that my husband was responsible for it. Instead, I admitted, "You were right, Kels. Shad isn't going to ever love me like he loved her."

I bust out with tears, covering my face as my knees got weak. I never meant to break down this way and I hated that my sister was seeing me so helpless right now. When it came to Rashad and what we had been going through lately, I just wanted to pretend I was strong, and that nothing went on with him that I couldn't handle.

Yes, I almost lost my sanity in the hospital after giving birth, but besides that, I never wanted anyone to think I wasn't happy with him.

"Beauti, stop it!" My sister stated instead of consoling me and telling me that everything would be okay. Not once did she pull me in for a hug and after a while of me still crying and still nothing from her, I peeked through my fingers to see her sitting on the couch, not even looking my way.

I wanted to stop crying and go off on her ass, but I couldn't. My heart had been ripped apart already and I had no energy to fight with her.

Finally, after what seemed like forever, I was able to stop crying, but I remained on the floor. My voice was still shaky as I spoke. "Kelsi, why is he treating me like this when I'm his wife? He promised to never put anyone before me, but—"

"Because he's full of shit, Beauti, and you should've known he was going to do this. That man betrayed a woman he's been with for years for you, and you thought he was going to treat you better? I've been telling you how he was going to do you since you came to me and told me about ya'll. You're stupid and you're getting just what you deserve."

"What?" By now, I had jumped up. "I'm not stupid. I'm just in love. You're always kicking me when I'm already down. I don't even know why I came over here to talk to you. I'm sitting here bawling my eyes out and not once did you hug me and tell me that everything is going to be alright. You a fucking poor excuse of a sister"

"Well, you know what, Beauti. I'll rather be a poor excuse of a sister than a poor excuse of a whole ass woman. You caused all this bullshit and now you want someone to feel sorry for you. I'm sorry. You're my sister and I love you., but I don't feel sorry for you. Why would I, when this was what you wanted? I kept telling you that Shad didn't love you and now look at you, crying and stressing over that nigga."

I was now more upset that I had come over here to make amends and vent to my sister than my situation. I was never expecting her to be this cruel toward me and welcome me and my bullshit back into her life with open arms.

"You know what, Kels? Go to hell!" With that, I turned my back to her and headed for the front door. I had never been so full of regret in my life as I'd been the past few days.

As I was walking out the door, I heard her say, "I'll see you in hell when I get there." I slammed the door in response. It was crazy how she thought I was going to hell because of what I had done to Unique.

When I was inside my car and had my engine started, I pulled off like a bat out of hell, heading to my next destination. Since Rashad had clearly put me on call block, I rode past the house he had gotten for Unique. His car wasn't parked in the driveway, but I still got out and knocked. After ten minutes, I got back inside my car and just sat in the driveway for almost an hour, praying he would show up.

He didn't, and I left. This time, I went to his parent's house to see if he was there. His car wasn't, but I still sat outside the house and debated with myself whether I wanted to get out or not. While still sitting in the car, my mama called me, causing me to huff out a deep breath as I picked my phone up from the cup holder and answered the call.

"Yes?" I tried my best to sound as normal as I could, but I failed tremendously.

"What is wrong with you, Beauti?" My mama asked me, matching the attitude that was heard in my voice when I answered for her.

"Nothing, what's up? I'm kind of busy?"

"You kind of busy?" She repeated the words as if they were a bad taste in her mouth. "Clearly, you're not as busy as me since I'm still stuck over here with your kids. Do you even plan on coming over here to at least see them or bring them some clothes, milk, and diapers, or me and your dad have to keep buying what they need?"

I only sucked my teeth and shifted in my seat. My eyes rolled only for me to redirect them back to Rashad's parents' house. I was being a shitty mama, but right now; I wasn't in the right headspace to bring my kids home with me. Rashad had me stressed and the crazy ass thoughts that were once running through my head were back. I wanted to hurt him so bad and knew the only way I could was clearly by hurting Unique or one of his kids... Maybe Lovely since he loved her so damn much.

I didn't want to do anything to my baby, though. Just the thought of it had me on the verge of crying.

"Ma, not right now, please. I'm going through something. When I get time, I'll be over there to see them."

"To see them, Lovely? When you and that no-good ass nigga were on good terms, you came over here and got Bernard and kept him from me. Now that ya'll aren't and he got you going over to your sister's house, crying over him, you don't want your kids. You just like these bitches in the streets that think a child will hold on to a man." She paused only to add, "But you know what, just bring my granddaughter's medication over here and I'll take care of them. As a matter of fact, we can go down to the courthouse and you just sign them over to me. You do not have to worry about them."

She was so upset that after she said what she said, she ended the call in my face. My eyes closed as I sucked in all the air I could muster up and slowly released it. When I reopened my eyes, the tears I had been trying so hard to hold inside, made their way down my face.

Dropping the phone back inside the cup holder, I looked in my mirror and wiped my tears away before getting out and heading for the front door. I knocked and then took a step back as I waited for someone to answer.

I was happy when Rasheeda, my mother-in-law, opened the door. Unenthusiastically, I pushed a smile onto my face as I inched up some, closing in the gap that separated us.

"Hey Rasheeda, is my husband here?" I asked her straight up, not caring that she wasn't feeling my marriage. Not only did Rashad tell me she wasn't, but it showed on her face when she opened the door for me.

"Look, don't come to my house asking me shit about Shad. You got some damn nerve!"

Chuckling, I told her, "Well, I guess he was being honest. You're not feeling our marriage. All I can say is, join the club. You damn sure ain't the only one that's not okay with him marrying me, but just like I tell everybody else, you might as well accept it. He's my husband and we have kids together. If you want to be a grandmother to them and be in their lives, then you might as well suck it up and accept me as your daughter-in-law."

"Bit—" Before the B-word could leave her mouth good, she motioned toward me, only to be grabbed by her husband. Where he had come from, I honestly didn't know because he damn sure wasn't visible the short time we had been standing here. Rashad's dad had always been fine. He was the older version of Rashad and I used to always compliment his looks to Unique.

"Young lady, get the hell away from my door before I let my wife go and beat your ass," Rashad's dad, my father-in-law, told me.

Laughing, as I looked at Rasheeda, I backed away from her before I said my next few words, which were, "Girl, calm down. It's not that serious. You lucky it was your son that I married, and not your fine ass husband."

I laughed as I quickly rushed off the porch to my car. She was kicking and trying to break free from her husband before he was able to get her inside and close the door. Inside my car, I laughed hard as hell as I started my engine and sped off.

I continued laughing as I drove, feeling accomplished for what I had said at Rashad's parent's house, but on the inside, I was crying. I rode around for a while, riding back and forth by Rashad's house and everywhere else he was known to hang out, only to have no luck with finding him. Eventually, I just went home. It was dark outside now and I wanted to go ahead and get in the house, making a mental note to go see my kids tomorrow so my mama could get off my ass.

Letting out a heavy breath, I just stared up at the window in my living room. There was a little voice in the back of my head, telling me to leave and just go to my parent's house for the night. That would've been much better than going inside an empty apartment, but I didn't feel like dealing with anybody. Nobody but my husband.

I hated feeling like I needed to stay home in case he decided to bring his ass home, only for the little piece of heart I had left to break when he wouldn't show up. Saying fuck it, I reached over and grabbed my purse, and got out. Slowly, I walked up to my building just for me to get halfway up the stairs and hear my name being called from behind.

I froze, recognizing that voice from anywhere. When I turned around, Tony was making his way to me.

"Tony, not right now. Okay? I don't have time for no bullshit."

"I honestly don't care what you have time for. I've been calling you for the past couple of days. Why haven't you been answering the phone for me?"

"Because I've been busy, but why the fuck would I answer the phone for you when you couldn't even come through for me? I told you that I needed you to handle some shit and you failed at doing it." Throwing my hand on my hip, I narrowed my eyes and then asked, "I guess you won't be satisfied until I call your wife and tell her everything."

"Go ahead. She already knows."

"What?" My face contorted into a frown, wondering how in the hell his wife could've known about me. Tony and I had been dealing with each other for years, on and off. After a year of not dealing with one another, I contacted him, and we ended up sleeping together again. I only did it that time because I needed a favor for his ass.

So, after I had put his ass to sleep, I started taking pictures of me laying on his bare chest, some with my face by his dick and our naked bodies side by side. Tony just didn't know what I had in store for his ass, but he soon found out, not even a month later. I had his ass eating from the palm of my hands and had him doing whatever I wanted.

One thing about him, he loved his family, and I knew that... Hell, I even loved that he loved his wife and kids so much that he didn't want to lose them. It made him an easy target in my book.

"Yeah, she got text messages and all... So, the little games you're playing, you need to chill the fuck out. My wife even went to my brother when I asked her not to, and I've already told you that your girl is fucking with him. So, everything you had me doing is out now." Yes, Tony told me all about his brother, Dyce, and Unique, and I was shocked to learn that.

He was the total opposite of Rashad. Don't get me wrong, the man was fine as hell, but he wasn't what Unique was used to. Then again, he had money, so I guess she thought she had won a prize. *Child, please!*

I opened my mouth to speak, but the figure behind him caught my eye. When I looked past him, my eyes immediately rolled upward as I spotted Mrs. Sally and her granddaughter walking toward us.

Mrs. Sally smiled as she spoke to me, but I only turned around and started walking back up the stairs so I could get out their way, not even speaking back. I wasn't in the mood for her ass tonight. I had too much on my mind and I damn sure wasn't trying to speak to her granddaughter.

"Grandma, please stop speaking to that girl, because she got one more time to be rude to you and I'm going to beat her rude ass." Stopping in my tracks, I turned back around and scowled at the bitch that had just said that, asking her what the fuck she had just said—which, I heard her loud and clear. "Girl, you heard what the fuck I said!"

"Jordyn, baby. It's okay."

"Nah, it's not okay, Grandma. I'm sick of her walking around here like somebody owes her something."

"Bitch, I never said you or your grandmama owe me something. Fuck you!"

"Nah, I don't want to fuck you, but I'll fuck your husband again, bitch!"

I couldn't do or say shit. I was speechless for what seemed like forever. My eyes became blurry and before I knew it, I was trying to charge at her ass. Luckily for her, Tony was standing between us. Hell, lucky for her *and* her grandma because I damn sure probably would've pushed her down the stairs to get to her granddaughter.

Picking me up as I kicked and screamed, Tony carried me up to my front door as that bitch continued laughing and telling me how good my husband's dick was, as if I didn't already know it. I could see Mrs. Sally saying something to her, but I didn't know what she was saying.

"Give me your damn keys." Tony snatched my keys and unlocked my door. It was obvious which one it was being that it was only three on there. The key to my car, the key to my mailbox and my house key. He carried me inside and didn't put me down until the door was closed. "Chill the fuck out before someone calls the police on your ass."

"I don't give a fuck, and you need to get the hell out of my house before my husband comes and catches you in here."

"Nah, I came here to talk to you about the twins." He paused as I sucked my teeth and rolled my eyes. My chest was rapidly heaving up and down and my hands were trembling. I needed him out of my apartment so I could call Rashad and see if what that bitch said was true. Had Rashad, my husband, been fucking with someone else, I was going to kill him.

I had already given him a pass with Unique, but I wasn't about to tolerate him being with someone else. Now I wondered if she was the reason, he hadn't been home.

"Did you hear me? I want a test on them." Tony snapped me out of my thoughts. "Since my wife knows about them, I—"

"You're not getting shit, Tony, because those aren't your kids. They're Shad's kids." To be honest, I prayed both of them were Rashad's. I'd heard twins could have different fathers if they were born in different sacs and I had even read up on it. When I was in the hospital, I asked the doctor about it as well, and I was told that it was rare but could happen. I prayed it didn't happen this time, though I slept with them around the same time.

At the same time, I thought it was crazy that only one of them was born with sickle cell disease. Even so, I tried not to think about it.

"What the fuck you mean, they're your husband? Since when

you found that out because the whole time you were pregnant and even after you had them, you were telling me they were mine... even threatening to tell my wife. So, since when the fuck you found out they were his and didn't tell me?"

"Since my husband carried sickle cell traits, mothafucka, and my daughter has the disease." We glared at one another through challenging eyes.

He looked pissed, and I guess he had every right to be being that I had been pinning my kids on him to get what I wanted.

Tony was so fucking dumb and believed everything I said. He was a detective but was dumb as hell. I had been manipulating him for years, but I guess he was unaware of it just to keep his family intact.

Laughing at how stupid he was when it came to me, I said, "Tell me something, Tony. How in the hell could you even get a job as a detective when you couldn't even figure out, I've been using your dumb ass all this time? These were never your kids, and I knew that. I only told you they were because I knew I would need you again. I know how much you loved your family, and I knew there was no way in hell you wanted your wife to know you had kids. So... Ding. Ding... Maybe if you would've been on your job and got Nique sent back to prison like I wanted, then none of this would've happened."

"Wow... You really are a conniving bitch!"

"I'll be that, but this conniving bitch got your ass to do what I wanted." I paused for a brief second. "But, I might have another job for you. It all depends on if my husband goes through with this divorce. I might need you to get your team to do another drug bust, and this time, I'm going to make sure he's at the right spot, unlike last time when Nique's dumb ass had to take that charge for him."

I still couldn't get over how dumb Unique was. Although everything worked out in my favor, Unique was never supposed to have gone to prison. The drug bust was originally for Rashad. He wouldn't leave Unique for me, so I wanted to teach his ass a lesson, only for him to not even be home when I had talked to Unique an hour before the bust and she told me he was home.

I blamed the drug enforcement because had they been on their fucking jobs and been on time with the bust, he would've been home. However, as I stated, everything worked out in my favor because I married Rashad, and we had two beautiful kids together.

Laughing to himself, Tony walked up on me. I glared up at his ass, giving him a, *what the fuck you going to do*, look. It was crazy because I fucked around and quickly found out what he was going to do. He snatched my ass up by the neck, lifting my body in the air. He had a look in his eyes that scared the shit out of me. It was one that I had never seen before. Not on him or anyone else.

Not even on my husband when he was beating my ass for talking reckless about Unique.

"Bitch, I'm gon' fucking kill you!" His voice wasn't even the same. Tony sounded and looked possessed As he slammed me on the floor.

"Ahhhh..." I yelled as I quickly rolled over as saw the bottom of his shoe coming toward my face. He grabbed me by the hair, snatching me up and wiping me across the counter. In the mix of everything falling on the floor, my purse did also, and I hurriedly crawled to it.

I quickly dumped everything out of it as I was being pulled up by my hair. What Tony didn't see was the gun in my hand. Right now, one of us was about to die and it damn sure wasn't about to be me. Before either of us knew it, I spun around and fired one shot into his abdomen.

Tony's eyes widened as if he couldn't believe I had just shot him. Hell, I couldn't even believe it.

"You shot me, crazy, bitch!" I couldn't even find my voice when he said that and watched him as he walked backward and fell back against the wall. His eyes were low as he clutched his stomach while my ass was panicking, not believing I had just shot someone.

"Oh, my god... Oh, my god..." I whispered as I rushed over to my purse. I quickly threw everything inside and grabbed my keys that were on the floor beside it. Being that I had just shot this man, I knew I couldn't stay here and wait for the police to come.

"Beauti... I need help." I shook my head as I ignored Tony and rushed to the front door. Once I made it outside, I knew it was impossible to drive, so I did something I had no business doing, I bang on Mrs. Sally's door, knowing she was home.

"Mrs. Sally. Open the door. Please." I bang on it. When it was snatched open, her granddaughter was standing there with terror in her eyes with Mrs. Sally behind her looking scared as hell.

"Let me in... Close the door." I rushed inside. I was so damn scared. "I... I... I..." That was all I could get out as I busted out crying. It was obvious what I'd done and no matter how rude I had been to Mrs. Sally, she was still willing to comfort me, unlike my sister. She pulled me in her arms and rocked me, telling her granddaughter to call the police.

I wanted to tell her not to, even beg her not to, but I couldn't get those words out. As much as I hated Tony for putting his hands on me seconds ago, he needed help before he died, and lord knows I wasn't trying to go to prison for murder.

After telling Mrs. Sally and her granddaughter what happened, word from word, I just cried. Mrs. Sally kept telling me that everything was going to be okay, but how in the hell could it be okay when I had a man in my apartment fighting for his life?

"Thank God the police are here." Mrs. Sally's granddaughter stated. I hated her so much that I refused to allow her name to roll off my tongue, but that was neither here nor there.

"Mrs. Sally. Can you go see if he's dead, please?" I begged. Her granddaughter already had the door opened and was rushing out, probably running to tell the police I had shot Tony. Being that she had just revealed that she was sleeping with Rashad, my antennas were up, and I had in my mind that she was trying to get me out of the way just as I was trying to get Unique out of my way.

After what felt like forever of me sitting on the couch, rocking back and forth, and biting my nails, two police officers walked in with their hands on their guns. They called my name and when my teary eyes looked at them; I jumped up and got ready to ask how Tony was doing, only for them to overtalk me.

"Mrs. Russell, could you stand up for me and put your hands behind your back?" They approached me and one of them grabbed me and tried to turn me around.

"Wait... He attacked me first."

They weren't trying to hear that. As one grabbed my arms and put them behind my back, the other one said, "Mrs. Russell, you're being arrested for the murder of Detective Tony Walker. You have the right to remain silent..."

15

WHEN KARMA COMES KNOCKING!

Rashad Russell

I paced around Don's living room as he repeatedly asked me what was going on. There was no way in hell I could tell him that I had just killed someone without him asking me to leave.

Not only that, but I had set my wife up to make it look as if she had done it. My mind was all the way fucked up, and it wasn't because of what I had done to her, but because of the bullshit I heard when I was at the apartment we shared, and she didn't know.

Earlier, when I was here at Don's house, counting money, I got a call from my mama. She was fussing and cursing my ass out because Beauti thought it was a good idea to go to her house. When she told me about the disrespectful shit she was on, I was fed the fuck up. I'd been letting her slide with the slick shit she had been saying about my mama, but I told myself that it was ending today.

When I got off the phone, I told Don that I needed to leave and that he would have to finish the count himself. It wasn't like it was a lot to count, anyway. I know that nigga had noticed how much of the loss we'd been taking. I wasn't trying to accuse nobody or no shit like that, but I felt like Dyce had something to do with us losing money. We had excellent product, but it was no longer selling like it was.

Something was up with that shit because we never had issues like this before. It was one thing for him to disrespect me, but the fat fucker was fucking with my money, and I didn't at all appreciate that.

After leaving Don's I went to me and Beauti's apartment, and instead of parking in front of the building, I parked a few buildings down like I used to do when we first started kicking it.

After waiting for her for about thirty minutes or so, I went to the bedroom and laid across the bed, not expecting I would fall asleep, but I did, only to be awakened by a lot of commotion. I jumped up and grabbed the gun that I had set on the nightstand. Since I walked into my house and saw Dyce's sitting at my table, I had started carrying my shit more often now.

Just as I was about to make my way into the living room to see what in the hell was going on, I heard a man's voice telling Beauti that she needed to calm down. I stopped in my tracks, wondering who the fuck his ass was, but I didn't have to wonder for too much longer as I stood by the bedroom door, listening to their entire conversation.

A knife was jabbed into my chest to hear Beauti, my fucking wife, had tried to set me up. This was the woman I had married— the bitch I'd been sleeping beside every night while Unique was locked up. All I kept replaying was her saying the drug bust was one she had set up for me because I wouldn't leave Unique for her. It was crazy, and all I saw was red.

My trigger finger itched for her ass and the thought of making my presence known and blowing her and the nigga I found out was Tony, Dyce's brother, brains out crossed my mind. However, I didn't have to do that and when I heard the gunshot and Beauti panicking; I knew she had shot him. Yes, I heard the uproar from him beating her ass, but why in the hell would I help a bitch that tried to send me to prison and was still talking about doing it if I divorced her?

My plan of setting her up came into motion when I heard the front door open, and slam shut.

When I walked into the living room and saw he was still alive, looking at me and asking me to help him, I grabbed one of the throw pillows on the couch and smothered his ass until he was no longer breathing. The same way Beauti wanted to set me up, I wanted to set her ass up for murder, and I wanted to kill his ass off the strength that he was Dyce's brother.

The black ass nigga had played with me for too long and taking his brother's life was a damn good way of paying him back.

"Aye, let me use your phone right quick." I held out my hand for Don's phone. He reached over to the table and grabbed it, passing it to me. I wasted no time dialing Unique's number since she had me on call block. When she answered, her sweet voice caused my heart to skip a beat. Yet, I remained calm as I took a seat to talk to her. "Nique, hear me out…"

"Who is this?" I knew damn well she recognized my voice. We had been together for ten years, so how could she have forgotten it? Nonetheless, I told her it was me. "What do you want? Why the hell are you calling me?"

"Because I'm moving out of Atlanta, and I wanted to see you before I left. Just to talk. No strings attach and no bullshit. I just have to get some shit off my chest before I go."

"No, I don't have time for no bullshit with you, and please don't contact me again." With that, she ended the call in my face. I ran my hand over my mouth as I removed the phone from my ear. I had fucked up with her bad and the shit was driving me insane.

When I tried to call her back, she had already put Don's number on call block. I was pissed and had it been my phone, I would've thrown it against the wall. "Fuck. Here, man!"

With a shake of my head, I pulled my phone out and called Jordyn. She didn't answer the first call, but when I called back, she picked up. I felt nervous as hell to even talk to her, but I tried my best to sound normal.

"Can you talk?" I whispered on the phone as I quickly walked out of Don's living room and out the front door. I didn't need him hearing shit, I had to say.

"Um, I guess I can. What's up?" Her voice was unpleasant, and I prayed I didn't fuck shit up with her, especially when we talked about me moving out of town with her.

"You guess... Damn, you going to do me like that."

"A lot just happened, and I just need to process some things."

"I feel you, but can we just meet somewhere and talk?" She was hesitant but finally said yes. Being that I had just taken her, yesterday, to the house I used to share with Unique, she already knew how to get there, so I told her to just meet me there. I then went back into Don's house and told him that I was leaving. We dapped one another up and I was gone.

Pulling up to my house, I watched my surrounding as I got out and went inside. I took my gun from my waistband before going in. Since I walked in empty-handed to a guest in my home, I've been doing that. I wasn't about to be caught slipping like that again.

Slowly walking inside, I inspected my house with my gun pointed in case I had to blow a son of a bitch's head off. Another thing that had me edgy was the fact that I had just killed the mothafuckas' brother. I didn't feel he knew this soon, but I could never be too sure.

Sitting on the couch, I set my gun on the coffee table and started rolling a blunt as I replayed the conversation in my head, making a mental note to get a DNA test done on my kids, or at least on Bernard. I always found it odd that he wasn't born with sickle cell and his sister was. I guess that's why my bond wasn't as strong with him as it was with Lovely, because of the doubt that was engraved in the back of my mind. Yeah, the doctor explained that it could happen being that they were born in two different sacs, but I wasn't buying that bullshit.

Clearly, the woman I thought I loved wasn't shit and couldn't be trusted. So, regardless of if I thought they were my kids or me having doubts about one of them, I was getting a fucking test done.

Deep in my thoughts, the knock being heard on my front door caused me to quickly grab my gun. I had already finished rolling my blunt and was puffing on it, but I put it out as I got up to open the door.

I was sure to look out the peephole first. When I saw it was Jordyn, I quickly opened the door, pushing a smile onto my face as I stepped back and welcomed her inside.

"Thanks for coming," I told her. The smile she gave me back wasn't anything like the warm and welcoming one she usually had when she was with me, and I didn't know why. So, I asked if she was okay.

"Not really…" She shook her head. "Your wife got arrested tonight, Shad."

I dropped my head as she strangely eyed me when she stated that. I was afraid if I looked at her for too much longer, it would show that I didn't give a fuck.

"She shot someone, but she said he was alive when she ran across the hall to my grandma's apartment." I brought my head back up to look at her, feeling like a fucking fool that my dumb ass didn't even look to see if Beauti's car was parked outside or not. Being that she didn't fuck with Mrs. Sally like that anymore or liked Jordyn's ass, I would've never guessed she went across the hall to that apartment. "I can't even believe it was Dyce's brother that she killed. Then I had to be the one that called and told him."

I clenched my teeth when she expressed that. The fact that she was still contacting that nigga had me tight. The way I saw it, she should've lost all contact with him when she saw how he disrespected me back at the restaurant, but I was going to dead that shit once we made this move.

"Man, to be honest with you, I didn't even call you here to talk about all that. I know we're supposed to be moving—"

"Yeah, about that. My grandma isn't feeling it. I told you that I'll get her onboard with it, but nah... It's not happening, and to tell you the truth, I don't think it's going to happen after tonight." Jordyn hopped off my couch as if she had ants in her gotdamn pants, grabbing my gun in the process. It happened so fast that it confused the fuck out of me.

"Yo', what the fuck are you doing?" I stood, still confused by her holding my gun. Instead of her saying anything, she walked over to my back sliding door and unlocked it. I took three steps her way before my movement came to a halt and I realized what in the fuck was going on.

I looked from Jordyn to Dyce's big ass walking through my sliding door, to Ta entering behind him. They were both mugging the fuck out of me while Jordyn had a blank expression coating her face.

"Man, what the fuck is going on? Jordyn, give me back my shit." I held out my hand as if she would really give me back my gun. It was clear what was going on, especially when she had just sat here and said she had called Dyce and told him that Beauti shot his brother. Still, I asked, "What the fuck are you doing? I thought we were—"

"Yeah, you thought, nigga! You were just a fuck!" Her words trailed off as she ran her tongue over her lips. "Somebody, I was using just to get over this nigga, but did you really think I was going to be with you after you let Dyce punk you back at the restaurant? On top of that, you're grimy as fuck, fucking with two friends. Yeah, I told you that I would still fuck with you, and I had no problem doing that, but it wasn't going to be anything serious."

"Fuck you mean, it wasn't going to be anything serious? We talked about moving back to—"

"Nigga, my grandmama doesn't even like yo' hoe ass, so what in the fuck makes you think I'll move anywhere with you? Me and my grandma are moving back, but fuck you!" I started to grab the bitch by the back of her hair when she turned her back to me to look at Dyce, but I had two niggas standing there, mugging the shit out of me. There was no doubt in my mind that I was about to die, but I didn't want to make it easy for their asses. So, I did nothing. Handing my gun to Dyce, she went, "Whatever happens tonight, please keep my name out of it. The only reason I even called you is because I loved Tony and he didn't deserve what happened to him."

I was confused by all this, because if this was about Dyce's brother and Beauti supposedly had killed him, then where in the fuck I came in at. Confusedly, I asked, "Hold the fuck up... How I get into this bullshit?"

Jordyn looked over at me and said, "Oh, yeah... I was at my grandma's house when you got to your wife's apartment. I guess you didn't see me when you parked a couple of buildings down and walked up to hers, but I was sitting in my car. Later on, I took her to the store and when we got back, your car was still parked in the same spot and your wife had got home. She was standing on the steps with Tony, and they went into the apartment after I was about to beat her ass for disrespecting my grandma. After she shot him and ran over to my grandma's apartment, I stood at the door with it cracked open, watching to see if you would come out because I knew you were still in there. Just as sure, you came rushing out and if that girl said the man was alive when she left out, I believed her. But, even if he wasn't, and she really killed him, sorry you're about to die."

"Bitch!" I didn't know what had overcome me, but I rushed to her only to be knocked back by a powerful punch to the face, knocking me the fuck out. I didn't know if it was the powerful blows that were being delivered on my ass that woke me up or what, but before I knew it, I felt myself losing consciousness again. The beating was too much to handle, and it fucked me up that before everything went black around me, I saw Ta just standing there and knew it was only Dyce beating my ass...

EPILOGUE

Love Never Felt So Right!

Unique James

Three weeks later...

There had been so much peace in my life, and I owed it all to Dyce. Not only him but Angie because if it wasn't for her, my ass would've been locked back up a long time ago. Angie had not only put her job on the line but her freedom and others' freedoms as well. Beauti had for sure taken a warrant out on me after I beat her ass, but my girl, Angie, came through.

She knew mothafuckas and had that warrant disappearing.

I cried like a baby when she told me that, but I didn't think my tears then equaled up to the ones I had when Dyce sat me down and told me that Beauti wasn't the only one that was behind me going to prison, which was still my fault for taking the drug charge for Rashad, but his brother was the one that had arranged for the drug bust to happen and he had been calling my probation officer, disguising his voice.

Angie cried along with me as she told me that she had nothing to do with any of the deceitfulness that her husband was on. That was something she didn't have to tell me because I already knew. She had looked out for me too much for her to have been in on anyone working against me.

Even so, no matter what her husband had done to me, I never wanted to see him die. It hurt me that Dyce was still hurting behind his death. Yes, he went on as if everything was the same and he wasn't affected by it, but I knew the pain was there. Just from the short time of me knowing him, I knew how much he loved his brother and sister, and to have one of them murdered was hard to accept.

Another thing that hurt him was that his father didn't even have the courtesy to come to his own son's funeral. That was just low, and Dyce, nor his sister, who I had grown to love, hid their anger about it. I didn't blame them because it was fucked up. Tony was his oldest son, so you would think that the man would be there. However, I didn't say anything about it, because it was a family business that I wasn't trying to get in the middle of.

After Rashad's body was found in his car with a single gunshot wound to the back of his head, it was hard to face Rasheeda, knowing Dyce was the cause of his death. The police knew there was foul play, but they had no suspects in custody and the case had recently turned into a cold case. Plus, it was drugs in the car, and they suspected it to be drug-related.

Since Rashad's death, Rasheeda and Mama B got together so she could meet the twins. Rasheeda made it clear that before she accepted them, although they were innocent babies, she wanted to make sure they were her grandkids. Regardless of Lovely's condition, she didn't like Beauti and wanted to be on the safe side. I felt she was secretly praying they weren't Rashad's, but after her and her husband used their blood for the test, the results came back that Rashad was the father of them both.

Now Rasheeda and Mama B shared custody of them. Mama B would have them for two weeks, and then Rasheeda would have them for two. I was happy they worked it all out, especially since their mama was never getting out of prison. She had killed someone on the police force, so they were trying to give her the max, no matter how much she cried it was self-defense and he wasn't dead when she left out.

Did I feel sorry for Beauti? Hell to the no!

Yet, I felt sorry for the babies, though. Luckily, they had two wonderful sets of grandparents.

Kelsi, on the other hand, I hadn't really heard from her besides her and Ta was no longer fucking around anymore, and he was the one that had told me that, of course. I still didn't have shit to say to that bitch and she knew it.

Ta got tired of their situation, and that was understandable. He was in love with the girl, and she kept curving him. So, I was happy he had moved on if she didn't want his ass. There was no need to waste his time on a bitch that obviously didn't want him.

On the good side, Dyce and I were going great, and we had just found out that I was pregnant. This time, the baby was his, and we were both ecstatic about it. God knows I prayed for this moment. With my first pregnancy, I couldn't enjoy it being that I didn't want to be pregnant by Rashad's ass.

Although I was only a month, I knew I would be able to enjoy this one to the fullest with my man...

I was now staying with Dyce and had been for three weeks. He asked me to move in over a candlelight dinner, the same night his brother was killed. As a matter of fact, our dinner was cut short due to his ex blowing up his phone. The heifer was calling so much that I just told Dyce to answer it and see what she wanted.

He did, and he put it on speaker since we were the only ones in the restaurant. Yes, he had rented the place out for us. When he answered, the words that came out of his ex's mouth caused my heart to drop to my stomach. She explained how Beauti shot Tony, but she also told him that Rashad rushed out of the apartment, too.

After hearing that, even with me not knowing who really killed his brother, I knew there was no saving Rashad, and I didn't even try. Dyce had been trying to spare the man for the sake of me, but that shit was off the table now, and I knew it was. To make matters worse, Rashad's ass had the nerve to call me when Dyce was taking me back to my hotel. I put the phone on speaker as soon as I heard his voice.

When we pulled up to the hotel, Dyce didn't even get out, and I didn't ask him to. In fact, I told him to go handle his business but make it back to me safely, before giving him a long kiss and telling him I loved him. I was asleep with he got back to the hotel and because he had a key card, he let himself in. I awakened to him in the shower and joined him where we made love as we professed our love for one another.

All night, the man sexed me like he never had before. I felt all the love he had for me, and it made me realize that for ten years, the love I thought Rashad had for me wasn't love at all. This was love! This was the love I had always longed for... A love that I didn't even know I needed. Everything with Dyce felt so right, and I had faith that a love like ours was going to last.

THE END!!!

Made in the USA
Columbia, SC
30 April 2023